CHARLOTTE (SPECIAL FORCES: OPERATION ALPHA)

FINDING HIS DESTINY BOOK ONE

ANGELA RUSH

Dear Readers,

Welcome to the Special Forces: Operation Alpha Fan-Fiction world!

If you are new to this amazing world, in a nutshell the author wrote a story using one or more of my characters in it. Sometimes that character has a major role in the story, and other times they are only mentioned briefly. This is perfectly legal and allowable because they are going through Aces Press to publish the story.

This book is entirely the work of the author who wrote it. While I might have assisted with brainstorming and other ideas about which of my characters to use, I didn't have any part in the process or writing or editing the story.

I'm proud and excited that so many authors loved my characters enough that they wanted to write them into their own story. Thank you for supporting them, and me!

READ ON!

Xoxo

Susan Stoker

NOTE TO THE READER

Hello, thank you for taking the time to read my book. If you are a fan of Susan Stoker's SEAL of Protection series, you will recognize some of the characters in this story. I have tried to be true to her characters as much as possible. However, I am not Susan. She is an amazing author and I hope that I have given Wolf's team and their women justice in my story telling.

I want to give full disclosure. This is a work of fiction. I have no military background or ties to the military. This book is intended to be for entertainment only. I will warn you I may not always use the correct terms true military personnel would use and my characters take more liberties than a true member of our nation's great military would do in a real-life situation. While I have tried to research and use correct rank, chain of command, and terms I will not say that those of you who are intimate with the military may not find me lacking.

I respect our men and women who have taken the oath to protect our country and our rights as citizens of this amazing country that we are privileged to live in. I am so thankful for all who have served and their families that serve along side them. As civilians we often go about our day not thinking about their daily sacrifice.

May God Bless America and wrap a layer of protection around our brave men and women that serve both at home and abroad. Remember Everyone Deployed. May they all come home.

Thank you

To Susan Stoker - Thank you so much for the opportunity to tell this story and your willingness to allow me to include your very awesome characters in my book. You are an amazing author with a seemingly endless number of stories to tell. Each one engaging and educating. I love how you not only tell a love story, but also give us insight into many social issues that plague our great country and world in general. I will be forever grateful to you for this amazing opportunity to put my story in print.

Thank you to my family and friends for the encouragement and patience while I was writing and revising and revising this book. It has been a dream of mine for many years to put my ideas into print and I am forever grateful for your support during this endeavor.

To my husband, Johnny thank you for all your love and support during our marriage and especially during the recent trials in our lives. We have had good times and bad, but you have always been a source of love and support. I am so thankful to have you in my life, by my side, and in my heart.

To my children, Beth, Erin, and John thank you for loving your crazy mother and tolerating her being distracted and engrossed in her books. You are all amazing and I am proud to be your mother. Please don't ever hold back and reach for your dreams, they can come true.

CHAPTER 1

CHARLOTTE

Working my way down the concourse of the international airport is proving to be more difficult than I anticipated. My left shoulder flies backward as a very large and obviously in a hurry businessman in his three-piece suit slams into me as he passes me, dragging his rolling suitcase behind him. I'm here three hours early for several reasons. First, I want to beat the rush hour traffic as I am on an early flight. Second, I like to make sure I have plenty of time to get through security and not have to rush for my terminal gate. Third, I just need some time to myself.

Being widowed at the age of 37 due to the unexpected heart attack of my husband in the middle of the night was not something I had been prepared for. Now at 42-years-old I have been feeling like half my life is over. What have I done with it? What great accomplishments have I achieved? Yes, I have two wonderful, successful children, but I feel like there was so much more I could and should do. So, at the insistence of a colleague, Dr. Jones, I have decided to take off work for a few weeks and go on a medical mission trip to help people in foreign countries receive much needed health care.

I have grown up and lived all my life in a small town in Kentucky, this is all new to me. Traveling out of country is an entirely new experience. Add the fact that I'm not traveling with any family is very out of character for me. My children are grown and have been living on their own for few years now. Without someone at home needing my full attention and support, the empty nest syndrome has hit me hard. I suppose that is why I felt the need to venture out of my comfort zone and seek adventure.

Dr. George Jones (yes that's his real name) is the leader and organizer of this expedition. We have been acquaintances for a while now. He is tall around 6 feet with short blond hair and sky-blue eyes. He keeps his slightly round face clean shaven. He is a little overweight by most standards, but not to excess. He moved to our little town of Deer Run, Kentucky about 3 years ago to replace a retiring doctor. He has asked me out a few times and despite me turning him down, he has remained friendly. He's a nice enough man, but I'm just not interested in him. If I am honest, I haven't allowed myself to even think about being interested in anyone. Dr. Jones has been talking about taking a Doctors without Borders trip since he arrived in town. He spent several years in the Peace Corps right out of high school and goes on a mission trip with his church group every year. He has built this trip up in our minds as our life's great work, to help those in poorer countries that would not otherwise have access to healthcare.

I'm traveling with some of my co-workers on this trip. JoAnn Walters is a nurse that works with Dr. Jones.

I have known her since high school and we even attended the same nursing school. Lisa Winters is also a nurse and the last member of our party. She is my closest friend. We are soul sisters. We were brides' maids at one another's weddings. I was there for her during her divorce and she was my shoulder to cry on with I lost my husband. We have raised our kids together and know each other so well.

Our group left a few days early so we could take a couple of days to sightsee in California before heading south. I have enjoyed my short stay here in San Diego during the lay over on our trip to Guatemala. It might not have been a good idea to come to the airport alone, but I needed the time to myself. Other than my friendship with Lisa, I have been a bit of a loner, after becoming a widow. This group trip is going to push my limits of socialization. It's only been 2 days and my nerves are starting to fray. JoAnn and Lisa mean well, but they are smothering me. They think we must do everything together. Dr Jones has been over the top to want us to stay together, too. Perhaps he thinks we will get into some mischief if he doesn't keep an eye on us. I'm hoping it's because he feels responsible for us girls since he organized the trip, and not because he is hoping to wear me down into dating him.

We did get a little crazy at Karaoke last night at a bar. I was the DD even though we were taking an Uber. Someone needed to be sure we made it back to the hotel safely and to be honest I wasn't comfortable letting my guard down. I've never been much of a drinker anyway and being in a strange town drunk was not my idea of a good time. However, we had a blast singing our hearts out and since no one there knew us, we could be totally crazy. We sang several country songs from Miranda

Lambert to Loretta Lynn. Aces' Bar and Grill was very nice, and the patrons encouraged us. I think they thought we were all hammered. Everyone had a hoot at us singing coal miner's daughter since we were from Kentucky and had that southern accent.

We got several encouraging remarks from a table of men that had to military. They were all handsome and buff. I mean we are talking major muscles, here. They all looked like predators ready to stalk their prey. There were a lot of military guys around since this is a military town.

"Charlotte, the blonde hottie with the black t-shirt at that table over there is checking you out," JoAnn squeals loudly. "You should go talk to him." Joann elbows me in the ribs a little harder than was necessary. Before I could formulate a reply, Dr. Jones jumps in.

"Absolutely not, Charlotte. There's no telling what kind of diseases you would catch in this town." Dr. Jones virtually growls at me, as if I would act on Joann's suggestion.

"Dr. Jones, let her have some fun." JoAnn drawls as she leans into him rubbing her breasts on his arm. "She needs to live a little." JoAnn continues to lean on Dr. Jones and giving him a show with her low plunging neckline.

"Something Ajax won't take off." Lisa smirks at me and then giggles. I can't keep the laugh from escaping my lips. Because she is most likely correct. Everyone has heard stories about women throwing themselves at military men especially around bases where SEALs and other Special Forces soldiers were located. They wanted bragging rights that they had slept with a badass military man.

After that fiasco of a conversation, JoAnn and Lisa

talked me into singing Miranda Lambert's "*Gun Powder and Lead*," as the grand finale. I really got into it, dancing around while I sang. The crowd clapped when I was done, but I felt like I needed to say something about the song. So, I went into my clinic speech when dealing with someone I thought was a victim of domestic violence. Who knows there might be someone in this crowd tonight that just needs encouragement to ask for help or say something to a friend they are worried about?

"Thank you all for allowing me to let your ears bleed with my screeching. But I would like to say a little something about the theme of that song. That song is meant to be entertaining, but it carries a serious message. I would never condone the violence this song suggests unless it is in self-defense. If you are in this type of situation, I would encourage you to seek out the help of a friend, neighbor, your healthcare provider, or police officer before you become another statistic in the news. Please get out while you have the chance. And if you are sitting there thinking this will never affect me. Think again, it could be your co-worker, your child's teacher, or even one of your relatives. Domestic violence spans all social and economic classes. So just be observant and look for signs such as change in behavior, inappropriate clothing for the time of year, and injuries with vague or unreasonable excuses. Speak up even if you feel uncomfortable approaching the subject. It could be the difference in life and death for someone. Thank you for listening, have a good rest of your night."

There was a large group of men and women in the back and they seemed to be having a great time. After our crazy karaoke session, I headed to the ladies' room. I had been drinking Diet Coke like no tomorrow because I knew once we got into South America that would be it for the next few weeks. While I was in the stall, I heard the door open and several women entered the bathroom. They were deep in conversation and didn't notice anyone else is in there.

"I will never get used to them leaving to go on missions." A female voice whined.

"I know, Summer I feel the same, but we have to put on a brave face for them. We knew what we were getting into when we got with Navy SEALs." Replied another voice.

"I really do try not to worry, but I don't know what I would do without Sam. Caroline, are we all coming to your house when they leave or are we going to Jess's?" Summer asked.

"We decided that we would gather at my house that night like always. There are a couple of ladies from the base that are going to keep the kids upstairs while we have a traditional 'get drunk cause our men are gone party'. Then Fiona and I are going to Jess's the next night to help with the kids. She has her hands full with the 2 babies so close in age." Replied Caroline.

When I finished my business, I left the stall trying not to be in the way of the ladies crowded around the sinks and mirrors as they carried on their conversation. I realized that they were talking to me while I was washing my hands.

"You should not go to the bathroom alone, especially in a bar. It can be very dangerous." A beautiful blonde lady said to me. "By the way I liked your version of "Gun Powder and Lead" and the comments you made to the audience afterward. So many women suffer from domestic violence and never seek help. I am glad you brought it up tonight."

"It is a subject that touches my heart. I have seen too

many cases of unnecessary injuries and death caused by domestic violence. If I can help one person get out of a desperate situation, then I have done my job and I can sleep at night." I replied to the women. "As for coming in here by myself, I haven't been drinking and I have taken self-defense classes. I know that won't prevent everything, but I try to be aware of my surroundings."

"My name is Caroline. Let us walk you back to your group. We never let someone go to the restroom alone and one of our spouses stands in the hall. We had the misfortune for some of our group to be kidnapped from this very bar while going to the bathroom." The dark-haired woman named Caroline replied.

"Thanks for walking me back. I'm sorry to hear about your friends. I hope they are ok." I said with a big smile. "By the way, my name is Charlotte."

When we exited the bathroom, I noticed there was a tall muscular man standing in the hallway watching the door. When we entered the hall, he stepped back and let us pass then followed us across the bar. The ladies walked me back to my table. Dr Jones declared it was time we headed back to the hotel before we did anything else that was too crazy. I think we must have embarrassed him. I was shocked as we walked past the table with the ladies from the restroom, JoAnn loudly said, "Charlotte I swear I don't know why you have to be such a drama queen and make a speech at karaoke. Did you not get enough attention as a child or something?" I didn't reply as I was shocked and a little embarrassed at her observation. I just lowered my head and followed the group out the door.

Even now after having slept a few hours her words still sting a little. Why I worry about what she thinks is beyond me and it's not like I will ever see those ladies from the bar again. Still, I wish she hadn't embarrassed me. There is a little café up ahead. I could use some coffee to help improve my mood. There is a line at the counter, so it takes a few minutes for me to get to the counter to order.

Once I have ordered and paid, the barista hands me my large mocha coffee. Several people are crowding the counter so when I turn to leave, I run smack into a hard wall of muscle. My coffee sloshes down the front of my University of Kentucky Wildcats t-shirt, and I would have landed on my ass if not for the strong hands that grabbed my elbows, steadying me on my feet. Once I am over the shock and first degree burn between my breasts, I look up into the most beautiful green eyes I've ever seen.

"Oh! I'm so sorry. I hope I didn't burn you with my coffee." I ramble to the handsome man who still has his hands on me. Suddenly my mouth is dry, and I can hardly breath. I hadn't been this close to a man in a very long time so I'm sure that's why I was acutely aware of the Alpha male holding me near him.

"No harm done. Are you alright? Did you get burned?" The man's deep rumbling voice sends shivers down my spine and goosebumps erupted on my skin. He was so close I could smell his sandalwood and male scent. The scent caused my lady parts to wake up and take notice.

"I'm f-fine." I stutter. What the hell is wrong with me? A man has never gotten me flustered like this before. I step back to get some distance so I can breathe when I bump into another customer. "Excuse me." I throw over my shoulder stepping back toward the man with his hands still gripping me elbows.

"You sure you're alright?" the handsome man questions again with a raised eyebrow. My nervous behavior is obviously not convincing. Taking a deep breath to steady my nerves wasn't the best idea. He scent was deeply embedded in my nostrils now. Somehow, I managed to get myself under control. Plastering a smile on my face, I nod to assure him all is well. He nods in return and releases my elbows. The sudden loss of his hands startles me, but I manage to move out of the way so he can move up to the counter.

Once I am seated at my table, I notice he is with a group of soldiers that had entered the airport café where I had decided to wait for my friends. After getting their items from the counter, they take their seats at a couple of tables off to my right. They are dressed in Army green t-shirts, camouflage pants, and combat boots. They are all tall, muscular, and handsome. Are they are heading out on deployment or just returning home? It would be nice to tell them I am thankful for what they do. Should I say anything to them? I feel compelled to thank them for the sacrifice of their time away from family and friends, but most importantly the fact that they willingly risk their lives for us mere civilians. After hearing the women in the bathroom last night talking about their SEALs leaving for a mission, I decide to bite the bullet and say what is laying on my heart at that moment.

It's go-time, so standing I make my way over to the group. As I approach the table, they look up at me and suddenly they all stand up. In shock, I take a step back but now I'm even more determined to say what I came over here to say. It's really nice to meet a group of true gentlemen. They are very intimidating. Smiling confidently (I hope) while shaking like a leaf on the inside, I lick my lips and take a deep breath to steady my nerves and gather my thoughts.

"You don't have to stand on my account." I say. "I hope you all hear this often and I'm sure it sounds cliché, but I wanted to thank you gentlemen for all you do to ensure the safety of our country. I can't imagine what horrors you see and do to allow the rest of us to go about our daily lives without a thought of what it takes to have the freedom we have here in the States. So, thank you again. I'll let you get back to your meal. I wish there was more I could say or do, but that's all I have." I ramble on like an idiot.

As I turn to leave there is a gentle pressure on my arm. An electric shook seems to run up my arm and settles in my chest. The heat of his hand on my arm is stimulating and comforting much like when he held my elbows to keep me from falling. He takes my hand in his as I look up into his beautiful green eyes again. He is tall, dark, and handsome. The man smiles at me and says, "Thank you for taking the time to remind us why we do this. It means a lot to me and my men." Then he places a kiss on the back of my hand. He seems to linger a little longer than is necessary. His touch causes a stirring inside that I haven't felt in years.

"You're very welcome." I reply with a smile as the heat of a blush floods in my face. Suddenly I hear JoAnn is calling my name. Looking over my shoulder I see Lisa and Dr. Jones with JoAnn hanging off his arm standing just outside the café. I excuse myself to join the gang before leaving for our terminal. I chance a glance back at the soldiers and notice that the man is still standing and is looking my way. Waving with a smile, I turn quickly and leave saying a silent prayer that those men will make it home safe and sound.

CHAPTER 2

HAWK

It has been a long day, hell, a long week. We are being sent to a Naval base in San Diego, California for a new mission. Thankful I am with my team. We have been together for the last several years. The men on my team are as close to me as my own brothers. Deadeye, Straw, Ace, Wallace, Tank, Worm, Virus, Mercury and Hack are some of the best men I know. Marine Raiders teams are larger than some other Spec-op teams in other branches of the military. There are ten of us in the field with another four members at headquarters. Captain Mark Olson is the commander of our team. Master Sergeant James Kellers, Gunnery Sergeant Robert Jamison and Gunnery Sergeant Erik Rafters round out the headquarters members.

We work like a well-oiled machine. Words are rarely required when out in the field, we act on instinct. We get the job done, everyone comes home, and then we throw a few back and put our feet up. Lately I have had this restless feeling that something is missing. I haven't been able to figure it out. I know that my days in the field will come to an end as I get older, but what will I do then? Can I sit behind a desk directing troops? I enjoy hunting and fishing, but I don't see myself retiring to a life of leisure. I've been on the move my entire adult life.

We have flown commercial to San Diego, California due to no military flights were available to get us here in time to join up with a SEAL team for a new mission in the Columbian jungle. Damn, I hate that place. It's not our first trip in that hellhole and I guess that's why we got chosen for this gig. We had barely gotten back to Camp Lejeune from Afghanistan when we got the word. It seemed we hardly had time to repack our gear before we were on the plane. Now that we are here, we have a couple of hours before the transport is supposed to be here to pick us up and take us to base. So, we decide to grab some coffee and a bite to eat from a little café on the civilian side of the airport.

Straw was giving us a detailed recounting of his latest conquest. It happened just after we had gotten back from our latest mission. We were only home for two days. When did he have the time? I swear that guy could pick up a woman in a convent of the elderly. It's easy to do when you don't have very high standards. Straw like the rest of us is only looking for physical release and nothing else. As a team we don't do relationships. It's too hard for most women to be tied to a military man, especially when that man is part of the special forces. We never know when we will have to leave or how long we will be gone. We can't tell them anything about what we do. After my disaster of a marriage, I'm not eager to try that again.

Julie and I had met when I was in my mid-twenties. We dated off and on whenever I was home. After a while she began to pressure me for us to get married. It didn't seem right, but I was nearing 30 years old. I wasn't getting any younger. So even though I had some reservations, I relented, and we married. However, after the wedding I came to realize she wasn't in love with me. She just loved the idea of being a Marine's wife. She wanted the attention she could get from Facebook. She wanted the sympathy from her 'friends' that she was sacrificing so much by having to sit at home while her husband was out saving the world. She was constantly making up shit to put on her page, whenever we got called up. Special forces soldiers can't talk about missions. Few people even know about the Marines Special Forces, much less where we go and what we do. She had caused me to be called in by my Captain and questioned about some of her posts. I warned her to stop posting stuff on there, that she could ruin my career. She apologized and promised to never do it again. A few months later, my team had gotten called up on very short notice. While we were gone, she posted all over social media that I was in Iraq taking out Osama Bin Laden. It almost cost me my career, but my superiors realized she was faking all the mess she put on there. We divorced, but she was already pregnant. That is another thing she was in love with the idea of, being a mother, but not so much the reality. Without consulting me she had stopped taking her birth control. After he was born, she decided she didn't want to be a mother.

I took a paternal leave for 2 weeks, before going back to active duty. Raising Brian was the most important job of my life, but I still had to support him. I loved my job and wanted to be able to retire from the service but was torn. The need to care for my son battled with my obligation to my team. After a long talk with my father, Brian went to live with my parents while I was gone on missions. My parents have a very loving relationship and have raised four successful children. I knew their home was the best place for him.

Leaving him the first time I was deployed after he was born was the hardest of my life. I missed him terribly and I felt bad that my parents couldn't have the retirement they deserved. It was better for him to have a stable home with his grandparents that love him, than to be bounced around every time I leave the country. Even knowing that, it didn't make this any easier. Especially now that he's a teenager, the need to be his fulltime parent has been weighing on my mind. Will I ever find someone who will love me for me and not my job, love my son? I have always wanted the kind of relationship my parents have, but perhaps it's not meant to be for me.

Having seen a lot of things in my 46 years on this earth, I thought nothing would ever surprise me again. I was wrong. Today I met a woman that did just that. I can't put my finger on why exactly. Perhaps it was her gratitude, her boldness, or the sincerity I saw in her eyes. I could kick my ass for not getting her name and number, but I was so caught off guard by my reaction to her, I just let her walk away from me.

The woman had literally run into me when we walked up to the counter at the café. She was only around 5'4" but she fit perfectly under my arm when I held her against me in an effort to keep her from falling on her sweet ass. She was overweight by most standards, but that just meant she had large breasts and hips a man can hang on to. Her voice had that soft southern twang that went straight to my dick when she spoke. When I looked into her gorgeous, intense eyes (brownish green with flecks of gold) I saw *her* and what I saw was amazing.

Later after we were seated, she walked up to our table. She was a beautiful woman to me. No, she wasn't super model thin or tall, but to a hardened asshole such as myself, I saw her beauty, what she is inside. Her curly brown hair fell down her shoulders beside a heart shaped face. It bounced as she walked toward us. I stood as she approached, and the others followed suit. She was wearing a simple Kentucky Wildcats t-shirt and jeans that mold to her hips, with a pair of worn looking tennis shoes. She seemed a little nervous, her eyes darted around to each one of us. She licked her lips while taking a deep breath. My eyes were drawn to her lips and then her ample breasts. Those simple acts had aroused me instantly, forcing me to shift uncomfortably as she proceeded to thank us for serving our country. I was trying to process why I felt such an attraction to this woman, when I realized she was about to walk away after giving us her little speech. I reached out to stop her and a warm bolt of electricity blasted through my system as my hand touched her bare arm. Taking her hand, I placed a kiss on the back it and thanked her for her kindness. Her skin was warm, and a tingle crossed my lips. They continued to buzz long after they had left her skin. She turned and walked away. Her hips swaying seductively as she crossed the café. My dick twitched again. It was getting uncomfortable. She grabbed her purse and carryon bag and left with a group of people. She spared a glance back at us. She smiled and waved before heading out into the crowded airport.

The guys clearing their throats and laughing brought me out of my trance. Looking around I realized I was the only one still standing. Deadeye, my closest friend and second in command, gave me an amused look, one raised eyebrow and all. I settled back into my seat and turned my attention back to my food and coffee.

"You want to share with us what that was all about?" Deadeye asked covering his chuckle with a cough.

"I don't know what you are talking about." I replied and continued to sip my coffee and eat my stale cinnamon roll, suppressing a smile. I stared straight ahead and ignored them. The guys resumed listening to Straw's story, and I let my mind wonder who this woman was and briefly wondered if I might ever see her again. Meeting her reminded me, I had no one to go home to at the end of a mission. Could I catch up to her before she boarded a plane? Get her number and give her a call next time I have leave. Why would I think that? I had no idea where she was headed. What had gotten into me? I hadn't missed having someone to go home before. Why now? I must be beginning to slip in my old age.

Now our transportation has arrived, and we are taken to base where we are introduced to a Commander Hurt and one of his SEAL teams. The men on his team are all well trained. They have been together for a long time just as our team has. It is easy to see they work well together. The team leader is Wolf. He is about my age and he seems to be well respected by his team members. We are introduced to the rest of his team. Abe, Benny, Cookie, Dude, and Mozart are all well trained men. They are all muscular, alpha men much like our team. It will be interesting working with them on this mission. I feel confident after meeting them that we will not have any problems completing this mission, safely.

The next morning, we are briefed on the upcoming mission. We are teaming up with the SEAL team to track and intercept a shipment of weapons and drugs destined for the US. A drug lord, Hugo Lopez has become a major pain in the ass to our border patrol officers. There have been several deaths along the border in recent months. Intel has indicated that the increased violence is linked to Lopez. He is known to be brutal and will stop at nothing to get his drugs and weapons onto the streets in US cities. He has an extensive network throughout the U.S, Mexico, and most of the south America. It could be a long mission, as long as several months, but with any luck we will be able to wrap this up quickly.

However, luck is not on our side. We spend several weeks gaining intel, training, and planning the mission to Columbia. It has been hard getting good intel. Hugo Lopez runs a tight ship. It has been very difficult to infiltrate his inner circle to get good information on his plans for shipping the drugs and guns across the border. We know that he won't be able to just drive them across without drawing attention to them. So, what are his plans? A man like him doesn't just blow smoke about such a shipment. He has a way. We just haven't uncovered it yet.

CHAPTER 3

CHARLOTTE

We board the plane without incident. Dr Jones and I are seated several rows from the rest of our group. When I ask about it, he says that he couldn't get tickets for us to all sit together. He laughs nervously and I wonder if he's being honest. Glancing back where the girls are sitting, JoAnn glares at me. Flying makes me nervous. I haven't done it much and with what happened on 9/11 it scares me. Dr Jones notices my trembling hands and reaches over to clasp my hand and squeeze it gently. He smiles at me reassuringly. He is trying to be reassuring, but it only makes me uncomfortable. I gently slip my hand from his.

"Don't worry. We'll be fine. I fly all the time, and nothing ever goes wrong," Dr. Jones informs me with a pat on my knee. When the stewardess comes by, he orders me a cocktail. I try to protest, but he assures me it will help me relax and not be so nervous on the flight. It does help, but I feel myself growing drowsy. Dr Jones leans into me and whispers. "Just lay your head over on my shoulder, hon. We will be there before you know it." It seems too intimate. I like Dr Jones, but only as a friend and colleague. He is making it clear that he wants more. How am I going to make it through the next couple of weeks?

We arrive in Guatemala several long hours later. The airport is a zoo. People are lined up everywhere, waiting on luggage, and to go through customs. Dr. Jones takes my hand to lead me through the crowd. Again, I feel uncomfortable, but I don't want to get separated from my group, so I don't argue. After what seems like forever, we have finally gotten our bags, gotten through customs, and we're waiting out in front of the airport for our colleagues. A shuttle bus is waiting to take us to the compound where we will be oriented to the plan for our trip while we are here. Dr. Jones and I get into the van when the others arrive, and we await them to board the bus after getting their luggage stowed. He makes a point to usher me into the window seat and take the seat next to me.

JoAnn and Lisa look worse for wear. I hope I don't look as bad as I feel, because if that is the case, I will look much worse than they do. Dr. Jones assures me that we all look rough after the long flight and trek through the airport. We finally arrive at the compound. Fear shoots down my spine at the site of armed guards at the gate. They look over our crew and check the luggage section. Our guide assures us that it is just a safety measure and is for our own good. I wish I had looked into this a bit more, done more research. Should I even be doing this? I didn't realize that we could be in danger from anything other than malaria or some strange jungle illness.

We spend couple days of in orientation that includes how to stay safe while out in the villages. It appears that there has been an increase in recent months of Americans and other foreigners being abducted for ransom or in the case of females being sold into the sex trade. Doubt fills my mind. Was this really a good idea? Is our safety worth the good we will be doing? After we get out into the villages, I see all the good we are doing, and I stop worrying about the dangers. The people seem eager to tell me their story. Over the next few days, I meet several young girls that are being used for prostitution. They have STD's, bruises, and broken bones. It is painful and heartbreaking to see them be treated this way. We had been warned that we might encounter such girls. We were told not to interfere, there might be repercussions, but I can't just sit back and let it happen.

"Dr. Jones?" He looks up at me as I enter his tent at the end of a long day providing care to the villagers.

"Charlotte, please call me George." I nod and continue.

"I'm very concerned about some of the young girls I cared for today. They need help. Several of the girls are being forced to be prostitutes." My voice cracks as I remember how the young girl had cried when I examined her and treated her. "I had a girl today that was only 13 years old and she had genital herpes. She wasn't the only one there were several others. Isn't there anything we can do?" My eyes pleaded with him to do something to help these poor girls.

"I have friend that works with the government here. Perhaps they can help the girls." Dr. Jones walks closer to me and grips my shoulders in his hands. "Don't worry about them Charlotte. I'll take care of it." I manage to pull myself away before thanking him for helping me save these girls.

JoAnn walks by as I am leaving Dr. Jones' tent. She scowls at me and I frown back at her. What's her problem? Probably just as miserable here as I am. The physical conditions are horrible. The days are exhausting and then trying to sleep on the ground in a sleeping bag is uncomfortable at best. Being too tired to contemplate her mood any longer, I head to my tent to sleep.

A few days later, the girls have been taken away by a humanitarian group. I was assured they would no longer be forced into prostitution. The clinic has been rough today. We have seen double the number of patients today than any day since we have been here. Word has gotten around about American's giving away medicine and treatments. A young girl of about 12 years comes in with second degree burns on her hands. She reports through the interpreter that she was cooking supper for her family when she spilled hot water on her hands. This happened 3 days ago. Her hands are red, swollen, and blistered. There are several open areas with pus draining from them. She has a low-grade fever. I give her a mild sedative before beginning to clean and treat the wounds. Burns are so painful, and I can't let her suffer through the pain of cleaning it this first time. After an antibiotic injection and some ibuprofen for the fever, I give the mother 10 days of antibiotics and explain how to give the medicine. Once the mother has been taught how to wash and dress the wounds, we give her the supplies she will need to dress the wound twice a day for 10 days. I inform her we will come back by the village again in a few days to check on her progress before we leave the country.

Later that night...

We settle into camp about 11pm local time. As I lay in my sleeping bag trying to relax enough to sleep, I again think of the handsome soldier I met at the airport. I wonder how he is doing and if he is safe. He has been on my mind and in my dreams since meeting him. It's surprising really. It's been five years since my husband died and I haven't once even considered dating, but if I'm honest I would definitely pursue a relationship with him if the opportunity arose. It's crazy to think like this. I don't know the man and I won't ever see him again. I mean what's the odds, right?

My sleep is fitful, and I dream again of the worst night of my life.

It's 3:02 am. Something isn't right. What woke me? I roll over and my husband isn't here. Did he leave for work already? I didn't hear the phone ring, calling him in early. Getting up I head for the bathroom. Unease plagues me. I need to go downstairs. As I descend the staircase. I see him lying on the floor of the hallway. He is face down and vomit spreads out from his body. Quickly I roll him over trying to clear his mouth. I shake him and shout. "David! David! Answer me, please!" No response. I feel for a pulse, he isn't breathing. I run for the house phone and call 911 as I race back to him to start CPR.

"911 what is your emergency?" the dispatcher asks. It's a very small town and everyone knows everyone.

"Carol, I need an ambulance now! I'm starting CPR on my husband. Please tell them to hurry." Throwing the phone to the floor not bothering to hang up. I begin to compress on his chest. There's no need to give her my address as it will show from the caller id on the system. Carol knows me. I work at the local hospital and have a private practice clinic in town. She knows where I live.

As I work feverishly to bring him back, I begin to plead with God. Please bring him back to me. I know I don't deserve him. I have been so absorbed in building my career that I have neglected him. I had been feeling the need to do things that I wanted. I have been a wife and mother since I was 17 years old. I had been feeling like I deserved to get out and live a little now that the kids are entering adulthood.

I know that I will never be the same. He has been my world since I was 15 years old. He's all I've ever known. He has been my only lover. The father of my children. What will I do?

It seem to take forever before the ambulance arrives. Terry enter the house and he pales at the site before him. James doesn't look much better. Sweat is dripping from my face onto David's bare chest. My hair is as wet as if I had just stepped out of the shower. My arms are aching so badly, but still I do my best to keep compressing his chest. Willing the blood to pump and restart his heart. The smell of vomit is strong in the air. Despite my fatigue, I begin to spout off orders.

"Terry get a line started. I'll get him on the monitor while you do compressions, James." I can't stop to think about what is happening. If I do, I'll lose it. I have to stay in clinical mode. It's the only way I am going to make it through what is to come. In the back of my mind, I know it's too late. He color is bad and if I'm honest I can see lividity where he had lain on the floor before I rolled him over, but I don't want to see that. It would mean admitting that he is gone and not coming back.

Once we have him ready to go and on the stretcher, I follow them out the door. Climbing in the back of the truck, Terry eyes me but doesn't say anything. They aren't going to tell me no. I see the fear and confusion in their eyes. I am too clinical, too focused. Not reacting like a normal person would at finding their spouse lying dead on the floor. I have emotionally checked out. James calls ahead to the ER to tell them to be sure the doctor is there on arrival that a code is in progress. Trying not to think about the implications of what he is saying, I relieve Terry from compressions. Knowing what is happening, I refuse to face reality at the moment. Doing what I always do when the shit hits the fan, I go on auto pilot, doing what needs to be done, emotions turned off. They can come later when I am alone.

Arriving at the hospital, the staff takes over. Jenny, a nurse at the hospital pulls me back from the stretcher as they move it into an ER room. They continue working on him. The ER doctor, Dr. Carter barks orders after getting report from the medics. My friends and colleagues work tirelessly to revive him. It feels like I am in a dream. Is this really happening? As I watch them, push drugs into his body and compress on his chest I know that it is futile. He died in our hallway. He is gone.

Eventually I come to myself and stop the horror unfolding in the ER. "Stop!" I shout. "Please...just stop." Dr. Carter, my friend and co-worker declares time of death 4:34 am. Damn we have been at this for an hour and a half. It seemed like only a few moments. I really had checked out. Thanking everyone for trying so hard, I receive hugs from all the staff. I refuse to let the tears fall. I head out to the nurses' station and grab the cordless phone. It's not time to fall apart yet. Our children need to know their father has left us for a better place. In shock I wait as the phone rings several times, before I hear Sara answer with a sleepy, "Hello?" This is going to be harder than anything I have ever done.

I AM JERKED wake sometime around 2 am to the young girl that I had seen earlier in the day at clinic with burns on her hands. She is frantic and is motioning for me to follow her. Through broken English I learn she wants me to come see about her friend that is injured a short distance away. Being half asleep still and not thinking clearly, I rise from my sleeping bag to follow her. I should have recognized something wasn't right about the situation. A guard should have seen us leaving and questioned me about where we we're going. No one stopped us as I grab my jump bag and head into the jungle with the girl.

We run through the jungle for several meters. The path is barely visible, and I wonder how the girl knows where we are going. Branches from the trees and ferns growing along the path seem to reach out and grab me as I run past, leaving abrasions and cuts on my skin. *Shit!* This was such a bad idea. What was I thinking? I should never have left the camp without telling someone where I was going. As I begin to think I should turn back, I'm shoved from behind as I pass a cluster of trees. I hit the ground, hard. Pain shoots through my body as the air is expelled from my lungs. A large man is suddenly on top of me pinning me to the ground securing my hands behind my back.

"What the hell!" I exclaim loudly once my breath returned to me. Struggling to get out from under the man, I only seem to worsen my situation by angering the man further.

"Shut your mouth, bitch! Don't fight me or you will regret it." A menacing voice growls in my ear.

Realizing I'm in deep shit, fear takes over and I begin to buck and kick trying to free myself. My jump bag is heavy and it's weighing me down besides the brute that is trying to tie my wrists together with zip ties. He becomes enraged at my struggling and hits me hard in the head with butt of his gun. It takes two licks before the world goes black.

* * *

WAKING to a massive headache with nausea and blurred vision, I feel confused. I haven't had a migraine in ages.

Why now when I'm in a foreign country in the middle of nowhere? There is no way I can handle clinic today with the way I'm feeling. I need to let Dr. Jones know and see if he can get me a shot of Toradol and some Zofran. The ground under me is hard and damp. I must have gotten out of my sleeping bag during the night somehow. My eyes refuse to open, something is not right. My face is swollen and stiff. My arms are bound behind my back in a very uncomfortable position. Suddenly it all comes rushing back to me. I was attacked in the jungle in the early morning hours. Where am I now? Who attacked me and why? What happened to the little girl?

The sound of voices nearby catches my attention. It's hard to make out what they are saying. I think it's Spanish they are speaking. Why have these men taken me? What do they want? Stay calm and don't panic. You need to be able to think clearly; I tell myself. My hands are still tied behind my back and it's hard to see anything. I need to figure out a way to get loose so I can escape. Raising up into a sitting position, nausea hits me hard and my stomach empties of all its contents in a few short minutes. However, my stomach continues to lurch, and I dry heave for what seems like an hour. The voices outside have quieted for the moment.

The darkness comes again. Waking sometime later I wonder if I have a concussion or a head bleed. If it's the later, I won't have to worry about what they are going to do to me. I will succumb to coma or death soon. Given the fact that I continue to wake from time to time, it's most likely not that bad. I don't think I've had a seizure because I'm not wet in my groin like I have peed myself. Sometimes it sucks to have medical knowledge. Ok I have to think, plan, get my act together and get my ass out of here before they come for me again, but I hurt so much. My fingers are numb, every muscle in my body hurts, and I'm so tired.

As I lay in the dirt my mind drifts to my children. They won't know what happened to me. Sarah and Justin have lost so much already in losing their father. I hate for them to go through this again. I am so proud of them. Justin recently graduated from the state police academy. He had gotten a degree in criminal justice from the University of Kentucky and then entered the academy. Sarah has followed in her mother's footsteps by getting a bachelor's degree in nursing. She is working at a regional hospital in the intensive care unit. I'm so proud of them. Neither has gotten married yet, but they will someday. Now, due to my foolishness I will never see my grandchildren. Why did I have to be so stupid? I knew better. We had been drilled to never go off by ourselves especially while out in the villages. And what did I do? Went off by myself with a stranger, no less and got myself beaten and kidnapped. Stupid, stupid, stupid! My angst is interrupted by the sound of footsteps and voices coming near. A metal door screeches open and I'm hit by a blinding light. The searing pain from the sunlight causes my eyes to scrunch together tightly. A shadow blocks the light. It's a large man with a gruff voice. He's yelling at me in Spanish. I only catch a word or two. I wonder if it's better if they don't know that I can understanding any Spanish so I weakly mutter "no speaka Spanish."

The man proceeds to kick me in the ribs several times. Having no way to defend myself with my arms behind my back, I take the full force of every kick. It hurts to breath. He has bruised or maybe even broken some ribs. God, I hope my lung isn't punctured. Again, it sucks to have medical knowledge. The man begins again in English this time.

"You are going to pay for your meddling, bitch. You should never have messed with our girls. You high and mighty Americans come in here and think you can tell us what is right and wrong! Those girls are ours! We will do with them what we want. It's what they are born for, to be whores, and serve my men. They are our women and you have no right to take them away and hide them from us. Where are the girls?" I don't respond. He kicks me a few more times. "Tell me, bitch. I know you know where they were taken. Where. Are. They!" When I continue to refuse to answer, he growls in frustration and gives me another couple of kicks to the stomach and ribs. "Since you decided to take from us, we will take you instead."

In my present condition, I'm unable to respond. My lungs don't have enough breath to speak and it's hard to think clearly right now anyway. The man, Asshole is his name in my mind, grabs me by the hair and drags me outside. I try to push myself along with my feet to decrease the pain in my scalp. They pick me up and throw me in the back of a jeep. Asshole and his companions, Tweedledee and Tweedledum, climb in and we head off into the jungle. I'm not sure how long we travel, because I drift in and out of consciousness. Suddenly I'm jerked awake by rough hands grabbing me by my shoulders and legs. I'm dragged out of the jeep and carried to small metal building with a stone floor. The men throw me to the floor with a thud and exit the little shed. The door closes to the sound of a lock clicking. I wonder if my colleagues have alerted the authorities. Is anyone even looking for me?

The days blur together as the beatings and moving from place to place continues. The men talk over me in

Spanish, not knowing I can understand them. I learn that not only are they in the sex trade, but also are involved in drugs and weapons. I need to get away. Struggling with my bindings only causes more pain. As I am faced with the futility of my situation, I let my mind wander back in time. Remembering the day at the airport when we were heading out on our trip I think of the man with startling green eyes and briefly relive my encounter with him.

As I turn to leave, a gentle pressure is on my arm. An electric shook seems to run up my arm into my chest and the heat of his hand warms my arm. I look up into the most beautiful green eyes I have ever seen. The man smiles at me and says, "Thank you for taking the time to remind us why we do this. It means a lot to me and my men." "You're very welcome." I reply with a smile. I can't say much more because this gorgeous man has stolen my breath away.

If only I could have stayed in that moment forever. I have let my mind think of the man often over the last few weeks since it happened. He has haunted my dreams, too. I wonder what his name is and if he has a family waiting for him. It's crazy to daydream about a complete stranger, but he stirred something in me that I thought had died years ago. My fantasies of him are the only thing that keeps me going through the days that follow.

My captors moved us several more times. I have no idea where we are or how far we have traveled from my base camp. Finally, we reach what I assume is our final destination, as it has been several days since we last traveled in the jeep. I'm kept in a shed with a dirt floor. There are no windows, so I am in the dark most of the time. It is unbearably hot during the day and very cold at night. They bring me water several times a day, but it is brown and gritty. It has made me sick; nausea, vomiting, and diarrhea has weakened me. My hands have been released from behind my back, but I'm kept restrained by chains on my wrists and ankles for most of everyday. I'm rarely released not even to eat or use the bucket in the room. My clothes are filthy and torn. Sores have erupted on my skin and I smell to high heaven.

When they come in to abuse me, I try not to show emotion. Knowing it will give them satisfaction to see my fear. The beatings seemed to come at regular intervals. It's how my day begins every day. A blinding light from the opening of the door of the shed, then they are beating me, humiliating me, and threatening me with worse abuse. Then I am left to my daydreams to pass the time until it comes again.

This morning some new men have joined the others. The light from outside is blinding. My eyes hurt so badly from the light. They have left the door open this time. Fear overwhelms me. There is something evil about the new commers. The group of men enter the shed and come to stand over me, blocking some of the light. Asshole is with Tweedledee and Tweedledum today. He seems to be the ringleader of their group, but the new men behind him are definitely in charge now.

These men are armed with machine guns at the ready. They have pistols at their sides and knives strapped to their thighs. The new apparent leader is tall maybe 6'4" with short black hair, a full bushy mustache. He is muscular and handles himself with confidence. His sharp chiseled features would have made him handsome, if not for the sinister look in his black eyes. He must be Satan, himself.

"Who's this brother?" Satan inquires.

"The whore I told you about that was meddling in

our business in Guatemalan villages. I was able to acquire her. Actually, I got paid to take her. Now, I am teaching her the consequences of messing with the Lopez brothers." Asshole replies with venom in his voice. He spits and it lands near my face. I can't help but flinch. Their laughter angers me that have given them any satisfaction.

"I haven't touched her yet, brother. I was getting paid to torture her, but that has come to an end. So now I'm going to use her. Would you like the first taste? Or do you prefer we train her first?" Asshole reaches down to stroke my cheek. I jerk back and swing my right fist toward his face, but the chain hampers my movements. So, I try to wrap the chain on my wrist around his arm in an effort to pull him off balance.

"You bitch!" He screams and smashes his fist into the right side of my face. Stars flash before my eyes and blood trickles down my face. I struggle to remain conscious, terrified of what will happen if I am unable to remain alert.

"She is filthy and fucking a whore in a tool shed is not my idea of a good time brother. You seem to have forgotten I have much higher standards than you do. However, she intrigues me, leave her untouched. Clean her up and bring her to the compound in 3 days. Then I will take her and train her myself. She looks like she would be a good fuck. Feisty, just like I like them. It's so much fun to break them." Satan says as he turns away.

The men begin discussing business. A large shipment of drugs and guns will be moved in a couple of weeks. The men are planning to attack a small outpost along the Mexican American border in a remote part of Texas. They know the shift changes of staff, the names of the border patrol officers, and their families. They are planning to abduct family members to get cooperation of the patrol officers. They are clearly insane. Can they really get away with something like this?

The need to get away and to tell someone, before they can carry out their evil plan is overwhelming. Drugs have wreaked havoc on so many. Drugs ruin the lives of not only the user, but their family members as well. The men continue discussing the upcoming shipment of drugs and weapons. They discuss which border agent families to target. They discuss who they think will be the most likely to heed their demands. Later the conversation again returns to me being held their captive. Satan seems to be unhappy that his brother has brought me here. He is rattling on about drawing unwanted attention to his operation. He promises Asshole serious harm or death if my being in there causes them to lose or get caught with the shipment of drugs and weapons.

A little while later after Tweedledee has given me my beating, he says, "It's time to have some fun. If we aren't going to get our money anymore, we can at least get something we want out of you. I don't care what the boss says."

He kneels next to me and shovels his hand up my shirt and begins to grope me. His touch is rough, and I can't stop a whimper from leaving my lips when he bites my breasts through my shirt. He pulls my pants and underwear down to my ankles and he forces me onto my stomach. I hear him fumbling with his pants. Oh God! This can't be happening. His rough hands grab my hips and jerk them up, so my sex is on display for him. I try to crawl away, but he is too strong. He holds me where he wants me. Just as I feel his vile shaft push against my folds, a shout from outside the shed stops him. Tweedledum enters the shed yelling in rapid Spanish. Tweedledee responds in a similar manor. They are speaking so fast I don't understand what he says.

Tweedledee jumps up righting his pants. He jerks me up from the floor and pulls my clothing back onto my body. Thank God! He again binds my hands behind my back and drags me outside by my hair. I am again thrown into the back of the jeep. The men seem to be upset about something and seem to be in a hurry to leave. We head off through the jungle at breakneck speed with Asshole at the wheel. I'm thrown around in the back of the jeep like a rag doll. My ribs are again very sore. It's hard to breath without coughing. As I begin to think, I'm going to pass out again, gun fire erupts.

My captors pull out several large guns and begin firing behind us and to the right of the jeep. Whomever is after these men are getting closer. Tweedledee and Tweedledum grab me roughly by my shoulders and feet. Suddenly, I am air borne. The ground rushes up to smack me hard. My head slams into the ground and my vision blurs. All the air is forced from my lungs from the impact. I look to see my captors looking back at me, but they don't stop. They continue to race away from me firing at some unknown enemies behind us. The roar of an engine fills my ears and realize that I am about to be run over by a vehicle that is hurdling along the jungle path.

I struggle to get out of the way in time, but it's no use. In my weakened condition and with my hands bound, I can't move much at all. Thankfully, the men in the Humvee that barrels down upon me sees me in time to stop before making me into roadkill. Several camouflaged clad men leap from the vehicle with guns raised and scanning the surrounding jungle. Who are these men? Have I gone from the frying pan to the fire? In my panic I can't seem to get enough air in my lungs and my vision begins to fade, the darkness coming in from my peripherals at a rapid pace. The last thing I see before I slip into the void is bright green eyes peering at me with concern.

CHAPTER 4

HAWK

We have been down here for weeks and finally we have a solid lead on the gun runner's location. We are loaded up and ready to raid their little hide out. We are taking 2 Humvees with my guys in the first vehicle and the SEAL team in the other vehicle. We head in first to secure the site and set up a perimeter. The SEALs will secure the weapons and ammunition and prepare for extraction once everything is secured. Everyone knows their job. We have been training together for a couple of months now and the SEALs are like an extension of our band of brothers.

As soon as we descend on the hide out, a jeep takes off through the jungle. Our group follows it in case they are going for reinforcements. Deadeye is driving while I relay to the SEAL team the change in plans. It is a harrowing race along a narrow trail. The green foliage whips by as we increase our speed in an effort to catch up to the jeep. We are at a disadvantage not knowing the terrain as well as those we chase, but it seems we are gaining ground. I hear gunfire and see the flashes from the end of a machine gun. I only catch a glimpse as the jeep careens to the right around a curve and out of sight.

We round the curve and see a long straight stretch of trail in front of us. The jeep is close. I can see the dark skinned, black haired men with guns blazing. Suddenly, they drop their weapons and reach down to grab something. Fear briefly races up my spine as I wonder if they have an RPG. When they raise back up, they throw something, no someone, out the back of the jeep and onto the trail. There is no way to go around the body due to thick growth of trees on both sides of the trail. Deadeye is forced to break hard to stop and not run over the body on the ground. The Humvee careens sideways as we slide to a stop. We jump out ready for an ambush. Moving to the body, I look down and see those beautiful hazel eyes that have been haunting me for months looking back at me before they roll back into her head.

It's the woman from the airport. The one that caused such a stirring in me, that I have found myself thinking about daily over the last couple of months. I have even dreamed about her at night, jacking off when I wake with her on my mind. She is covered in filth. Her clothes are torn and several shades darker than they once were from the layers of dirt caked on them. Her face is swollen and bruised in varying shades of blue, green, and purple. Blood oozes from a cut over her right eye and her lower lip. Her hands are secured behind her back with zip ties. There is fresh and dried blood on her wrists from prolonged exposure to the zip ties. Her ankles are secured in a similar fashion.

How in the world did she end up here? Why would the gun runners have an American woman tied up and then dump her out? Was she just a distraction to get us off their trail? She looks like she's been through hell. I pull out my Strider knife and cut the binding on her wrists and ankles. Being careful not to make her injuries worse, I slip my arms under her body and scoop her up bride style and carry her to the Humvee.

The guys are all watching me as I settle into the passenger seat with her in my lap. I cradle her to me as I bark out orders to load up, notify the SEAL team of our status, and to head to the nearest safe house with medical supplies. Deadeye my second in command takes the driver seat, eyeing me suspiciously. Once all the team is on board, he puts the Humvee in gear and takes off in the direction of the safe house. I know they are all curious about my actions. As their leader, I don't usually care for the civilians we encounter or rescue for that matter, but there is just something about this woman that stirs my interest. There is no way I will let anyone else care for her. Only me.

Once we arrive at our destination, I carry her into the bathroom of the first bedroom. Placing her down on the tiled floor, I turn on the water to the tub. She is covered in dirt and blood. Her breathing is labored and her pulse if rapid. Her clothes are torn in places. Deadeye follows me into the bathroom, helps me get her undressed and lowered into the bathtub. Keeping my arm behind her back along the shoulder blades to keep her head above water, I begin to wash away the grime. She would probably be mortified to know two strange men were giving her a bath, but it is necessary to get the grime off so I can see what kind of injuries we are dealing with.

As I wash away the dirt and blood, bruising in various stages of healing become visible. Her eyes are swollen. There are several deep abrasions along her forehead. It takes several attempts to get all the dried blood off her face. It has several lacerations and her nose has been broken as well as the busted lip. I move down to her chest and see the bruising of bite marks on her breasts. They look fresh. My blood boils and red flashes before my eyes. They have violated her. I will kill them all.

The feel of broken ribs as I rub the washcloth over her torso makes me sick. Large areas of purple discoloration covers her sides and abdomen. There is bruising in the shape of a boot print on her right lower back. She has fresh fingerprint bruises on her hips and thighs. Blood drains from her lower lips. Bile rises in my throat, but I manage to swallow it back and continue what needs to be done. I can't allow myself to think about what those men have done to her.

Once her body is clean, I reposition her to wash her hair. The water runs a brownish-red as we wash away the blood and dirt that is caked in her hair. She has a couple of deep lacerations on her scalp. They look like they have been there for a while and infection has set up. After we have gotten her washed and dried off, I carry her to the bed and place one of my t-shirts over her body and we slip some boxer shorts on her lower half for modesty.

Deadeye gets the med kit out and begin to dress the lacerations. Straw comes in and gets an IV started. He hangs some fluids and antibiotics. Using a stethoscope, I listen to her breathing to see if I hear any dead space that would indicate a collapsed lung. Feeling confident that we have done all we can for the poor woman, I settle in a chair at her bedside to wait and hope against hope we have gotten to her in time. It feels bizarre that I am this drawn to a stranger, but there is an undeniable connection to her that makes me want to protect her, keep her safe. I look to see if she is wearing rings to indicate she has someone waiting for her, but her left ring finger is bare.

"Hawk? You want me to take first watch?" Deadeye asks as he nears the bed.

"No, I've got her." I reply. He knows to let it be. Even though I haven't slept much for a couple of days when I set my mind to something there is no changing it. He shrugs and follows Straw out to help the team and make sure everything is secure. There's no doubts. The best men in the Marines are on our team. I never have to worry they aren't doing what needs to be done.

Time passes slowly as I wait for her to regain consciousness. Her breathing is steady, but I have noticed some rattling at times, and she has developed a fever. Using cool wash clothes, I wipe her down to cool her skin. We haven't been able to give her anything for the fever since she hasn't awakened enough to swallow any Tylenol. Worry has become a constant state for me. Will she live to make it out of here? Yes, she will make it out alive and back home, if it's the last the last thing I ever do.

CHAPTER 5

CHARLOTTE

When will this pain be over? I'm so tired of hurting. Why don't they just kill me already? What did I do to deserve this? I am basically a good person. I try to help others; I donate to the Salvation Army at Christmas and always get a couple of angels from the angel tree. I know I'm not perfect, but come on, do I really deserve this? I must have voiced my ramblings out loud, because a deep rumbling voice said, "No, love, you don't deserve what they have done to you."

My eyes fly open to see the beautiful green eyes looking down at me. I try to scoot away but I'm so weak my efforts are pathetic. The most handsome looking man I have ever laid eyes on, smiles down at me. Am I dreaming again?

"You are safe, love. Don't be afraid. I've got you." I'm confused. He is not one of my captors. It's the man from my daydreams. I look around to see where I'm at. The room isn't very large, but clean. There is a small window to my left where the sunlight is streaming in providing light. There are few furnishings in here. A table sits beside the bed and a few folding chairs are scattered around. I see an open door in the wall on my right that appears to lead to a bathroom. I'm in a large bed with the softest sheets, or perhaps they just feel soft since I have been sleeping on the ground for God knows how long. I notice I have an IV dripping into my left arm. It still hurts to breath, but I can at least get some air in my lungs.

"Where am I?" I croak. My voice is weak. My mouth is so dry. My throat feels like it is covered in shards of glass, it hurts when I try to swallow. When did I last have water? Or food for that matter?

"The Columbian jungle at a safe house." The gorgeous man declares. "I'm Staff Sargent Jordan Jackson, US Marine Corp, but my guys call me, Hawk. You are with a group of Marines and Navy SEALs. Can you tell me who you are and why you were laying in the middle of a trail in the jungle tied up and beaten half to death?"

As the bed dips down, I look to see the green-eyed man sit down beside my right hip on the bed. He is truly a handsome man. His black hair has smatterings of grey and is longer than I would expect a military man to have, but it looks just right to run your fingers through it. His face is now covered with a thick black beard and mustache again with streaks of grey. My gaze travels down the length of his body that is visible, and it is just miles and miles of muscle. I wonder if he has a 6 pack of abs. Large thigh muscles bulge and flex as he adjusts himself on the bed. As my eyes return to look at this handsome man, they stop at his lips. His lips look so warm and soft. What they would feel like against mine? What he would taste like? His thick beard and trimmed mustache cause me to imagine what they would feel like on my inner thighs as he devours me.

He is staring at me with his eyebrows raised in question. He did ask me a question, didn't he? And I was ogling him, having wicked thoughts. What is wrong with me? This is so not the time to be having these kinds of thoughts. I lick my dry and cracked lips to moisten them without success. He notices my feeble attempt and reaches over me to the nightstand and picks up a cup. He slides his arm behind my shoulders and helps me to sit up.

"Go easy, only small sips." His voice rumbles through his chest and into my body, doing wicked things to my lady parts. "You will get sick if you drink too fast." When I have taken a few sips, I tell him my story.

"My name is Charlotte Williams," I wince as I try to take a deep breath, but I continue. I tell him about myself, the girl, and the events leading up to my capture. "Once I realized there was no friend it was too late. I was ambushed, beaten into unconsciousness, and taken away. Wait! Did you say Columbia? How did I end up here? That's a long way from Guatemala, right?"

"Yes, it's quite a long way. When were you taken?" Hawk asked.

"June 2nd. We had been in country for about a week when I was taken." I reply. "What day is it?"

"August 20th."

"Oh God! It's been that long? Everyone must think I'm dead. I have to let my kids know I'm alive and my employer, if I even still have a job. Oh Lord! My bills and my patients at the clinic. Do you have a phone? I need to start calling people, "I rattle on until his laugh cuts me off.

Hawk chuckles, "Calm down. We will get word out as soon as we can. You need to rest and gain your strength so we can move you. We are still in enemy territory and we have to be careful with communication. We wouldn't want to give away our location and bring the drug lords down on us."

"Oh, Ok. I'm sorry." I whisper. Tears fill my eyes and begin to spill down my face as reality sets in. Shame cascades over me for being so careless. Why did I let this happen to me? Unable to hold back the flood any longer, tears roll down my cheeks. I have held my emotions in for as long as I can. Like a dam breaking, I begin to sob.

Hawk scoots closer and gently slips his arms around me. He lifts me to his chest and begins to stroke my hair and whisper soothing words in my ear. He is so gentle there is no way I can get control of myself now. Loud sobs escape my lips as I cling to him like a drowning man clings to a life preserver. It takes quite a long time for me to regain my composure. Once I have stopped sobbing, he raises my head and places his large calloused hands on both sides of my face wiping my tears with his thumbs.

"Don't cry, love. I won't let anything bad happen to you again. I promise, I'll keep you safe." His deep baritone voice comforts me as much as his gentle caresses on my face.

"Thank you, I sorry for having a moment. I so ashamed I let this happen to me. And I'm just so relieved to be away from those men." I heave a shuddering breath as I am still recovering from my episode.

"You have nothing to be ashamed of, love. Those bastards should be the ones who should be ashamed for what they have done to you." Hawk's face is a mix of sympathy and anger. While he can look terrifying, it comforts me. Looking in his eyes, I feel safe, knowing he is with me.

It should have seemed ridiculous. We didn't know

each other. Why would he want to protect me? It's just because it's his job, right? But in that moment looking into those gorgeous eyes, I felt like the most precious person in the world. There was no doubt he would be true to his word and he would keep me safe. Once the tears have abated, sleep claims me again as I feel safe in his arms.

* * *

Rough hands are groping me! The pain won't stop. I can't breathe and the fear is overwhelming. His fist connects with my face. Pain sears through my face at the impact. Now, He's removing my clothes. I know with certainty he is going to rape me, there's nothing I can do. My hands and feet are tied. I need help. I must get away somehow. Please, God help me!

As I jerk awake, I feel a warm hard body behind me. Fear consumes me and I try to get away. Where am I? My captors were never with me when I woke. Rough hands are trying to hold me down. I fight as hard as I can, but he is too strong and I'm too weak. Hearing someone calling my name, I try to focus on the words.

"Charlotte! Charlotte! Wake up, love. You're having a nightmare."

It's Jordan, Hawk, he's here with me. We're in the safe house away from my torturers. Instantly I relax in his arms. He must have lain down on the bed with me and fallen asleep, too. He continues to try and sooth me. He pulls me closer to his warm body and rubs his hand down my hair.

"You're alright, love. You're safe with me. I've got you. I won't let you go." He croons as he lays his cheek on top of my head. I sigh and snuggle in. It's been so long since I've felt safe and even longer since I've been held by someone. I know I shouldn't do this, but it feels so good, so right. I must have dozed back off to sleep, because a little while later I am awoken to my warm blanket pulling away from me and I hear voices over by the door.

"I thought you two should eat. I have some MREs for you." A deep voice rumbles from over by the door. "How's she doing today?"

"Thanks, Deadeye. She does need to eat. I'll wake her in a bit. The fever is gone, but she hasn't slept well. She keeps having nightmares." Hawk replies. I lay quietly and listen to them talking.

"That's understandable after what she's been through." Deadeye states after a pause he continues. "What's going on here, Hawk? This isn't like you man. You've never shown this much interest in a woman before. You haven't left this room since we got here two days ago."

"I honestly don't know. I'm drawn to her, her eyes, her smile. I just can't leave her. She's the same woman that spoke to us in the airport. Did you recognize her?" Deadeye shakes his head. "I knew the moment I looked at her on the trail who she was. I'll never forget her beautiful eyes. It's like it was just meant to be for me to find her again. I need to know that she is taken care of and while I know you guys would do right by her, I just need to be the one to take care of her, Ok?"

"Alright, as long as you don't let it interfere with our mission. We are here to take out a target. We haven't made any progress in the time we've been sitting here babysitting. The trail went cold and we haven't gotten any new leads, but I feel like you aren't concerned about that anymore. Your sole focus is that woman. She's not our mission, man." Deadeye declares.

"Dammit I know, Deadeye!" Hawk says sharply. "I

can't explain it. I need to make sure she is safe, protected. You know we can't just leave her here and we can't risk disclosing our location by using communications to get her out of here. Lopez's men are everywhere. I can't take the chance of them getting their hands on her again. She will just have to stay with us for the time being, until we can make arrangements for her to be evacuated from the country and back to the States."

"Ok Hawk, I trust you with my life," Deadeye's voice is laced with sincerity. "You know that. Just don't do something crazy that gets us all killed over a woman."

"You know that I would never do that," Hawk's voice is a low rumble as he tries to speak quietly. "I have always put my team first. Semper Fi."

"Semper Fi!" Deadeye replies with a chuckle. "You know that I will have your six, Hawk. I will do whatever you ask of me."

"I know," Hawk replies. "I am in your debt always. Help me take care of her? I trust you like a brother. She's means something to me."

"Ok, Hawk. I'll help you, man." Deadeye states. "The SEAL team is trying to gather more intel on this group. They have a satellite phone that can't be intercepted by the gun runners. They have reached out to a friend of theirs. John 'Tex' Keegan. He's a medically retired former SEAL and some kind of computer genius. Wolf said it's fucking scary the shit this guy can do with technology. Hopefully we will know more soon."

Hawk walks over to the bed and brushes my hair back from my face and places a gentle kiss on my forehead. He settles back into bed with me. He wraps his arms around me and pulls me close. I sigh because it feels so good. Why would this big badass Marine want to take care of me? I have no idea, but I'm going to let him for now. I'm just to tired, sore, and hurt to fight it. However, I can't let these brave men get hurt on my account though. So, if it comes down to them getting injured or killed and me going back to my kidnappers. I will have to go back. No questions asked. As bad as it was, somehow knowing that I caused the man behind me to be hurt would be worse than anything I would endure at the hands of my captors.

Hawk gently shakes my shoulders. "Wake up, love. You need to eat." I open my eyes and look into his intense gaze. It takes my breath to think about what he had said to Deadeye. I try to sit up, but I'm still weak and awkward. He helps me to sit and starts to arrange the food on the tray so we can eat. He takes a fork and scoops up some rice and vegetables. Shock rolls through me when he lifts it to my mouth. He's feeding me. Opening my mouth, I take in the food. It is really good and warm. It's the first real food I have had in months. After only a few bites nausea rears its ugly head. Pushing the food away to stifle the bile rising in my throat, I shake my head in protest.

"You haven't eaten much." Hawk states with a tone of reprimand in his voice.

"I just can't. It's making me feel sick and I don't want to throw up what I have managed to take in."

"Ok. We can try again later. Now we need to get you to the bathroom so you can get cleaned up." Hawk replies. He begins to clear the food away and untangle the blanket from around my body.

"But you haven't eaten." I say. "You need to eat too."

"I'm fine. I had eaten earlier while you were sleeping. I've had enough. Besides you will feel better after a bath and getting your hair washed. I know ladies are obsessive about their hair." He winks and laughs softly. "I haven't washed it since the day we got here and I'm sure you wash it more often than that, but with your broken ribs I didn't want to have to move you too much."

"You washed my hair!" I exclaim as my face flushes with heat wondering just how much of me, he saw.

"Yes, and the rest of you the day we got here. I had to see where you were hurt, and I couldn't with all the dirt, blood, and debris on you. I've only done the basics since." Hawk replies without any remorse in his tone. I blush profusely and make a noise of protest. "Look, I know you are probably shocked that strangers gave you a bath while you were unconscious, but I promise you that Deadeye and I were respectful of you. We only did what we had to do in order to take care of your injuries."

I sit in silence while I contemplate what he has revealed. While my rational mind knows what he said it true, I am still freaked out that he has seen me naked. My face is flushed. My breathing is rapid and shallow. It's like I'm a teenager again meeting a boy for the first time. His hand touches my chin and raises it, so that I'm forced to meet his gaze.

"I'm not sorry I did what needed to be done, love, but I am sorry that you are upset about it." Hawk states in a soft voice that is filled with an emotion I can't fully comprehend.

"It's…it's ok." I whisper. "I was just surprised and a little embarrassed. No one has bathed me since I was a small child. I'm supposed to be the caregiver not the recipient."

"Nothing to be embarrassed about. Even in the condition you were in, I was hard as brick while I bathed you. I know that sounds unprofessional, but I couldn't help how my body was responding to yours." Hawk confesses.

Now my face is on fire. I have never had a man express himself to me so bluntly. The fact that it's a Marine with a body to rival Adonis is even more overwhelming. I'm afraid I'm going to pass out if I don't get my breathing under control. Sucking a deep breath in, I hold it for a moment. Huffing it out, I blurt out the first thoughts that come to my mind.

"You can't say things like that to me when you are supposed to be taking me to get a bath. I won't be able to think of anything else except your hard on while I'm in the bath." My voice has risen almost to a squeak by the last sentence.

Hawk belly laughs. "It's good to know you will be as uncomfortable during your bath as I will be."

He proceeds to help me up, ignoring my protests. I can't believe the pain in my chest as I move. The broken ribs obviously have not healed much. Hawk removes my IV fluids and flushes some saline through the line and clamps the lock on the remaining tube left in my arm. Supporting my weight, he leads me to the small bathroom. Without saying a word, he slides the boxer shorts down my legs. He taps my leg for me to step out of them. I can only follow his directions. I can't speak or even think with him this close to me removing my clothes. He helps me to sit on the toilet and then turns his back.

"I'm sorry to not give you the privacy I'm sure you want, but I'm not taking a chance on you passing out again and hitting your pretty little head. It's had enough damage to last a lifetime." Hawk says. He reaches into the bathtub and turns the water on. "Bath or shower?" he inquires as he checks the water temperature with his hand.

"Shower." I reply weakly.

It takes a minute for me to be able to pee with an

audience, but once I'm done, he reaches for the hem of the t-shirt I'm wearing. "Arms up!" he commands. I comply and feel my nipples harden at the sudden draft that wafts over them in the cool room. "Stay." He again commands. He is taking his clothes off! There is no air in this room. My breaths are shallow and rapid as I watch his clothes come off. I shouldn't be looking, but I can't tear my eyes away. His body is bulging with muscles. It's even more magnificent than I had imagined in my dirty dreams.

His large pectoral muscles standout from his chest. They ripple with his every movement. He has an 8 pack of abs that beg to be touched and they lead down to a V that disappears into his underwear. His thigh muscles ripple as he removes his underwear. Trying not to stare at his dick, I am in awe at how magnificent he is. He is large in comparison to what I have had experience with. He notices me staring.

"I know this is awkward, but we would make a colossal mess if I kept my clothes on while giving you a shower." Hawk explains as he lifts me up and sets me into the warm spray of the shower. I should protest that I can do it myself, but why would I do that?

Once I am steady on my feet, he steps in behind me. He pushes me back into the down pour of water to wet my hair. He turns me so my back is to him and he begins to lather my hair with shampoo. It feels so good to have someone wash my hair. My body is reacting to the intimate act violently. I begin trembling and I'm not sure how much longer I will be able to stand. Placing my hands on the side of the shower to steady myself, I feel him move closer to me. He puts his arm around me and holds me next to his body as he gently soaps me from head to toe. Once he has rinsed my body and hair, he quickly washes himself and his hair. He reaches behind me to turn off the water. Then he grabs a towel and begins to dry me off then himself. He picks me up as I begin to falter and steps out of the tub. Sitting me on the toilet while he places a clean t-shirt over my head and slips some clean boxer shorts on me.

"Are you alright?" he asks concerned. I just nod. I don't have it in me to speak. I can't believe how tired I am from just taking a shower and I didn't even do anything.

"I'll be right back I just need to get my clothes on." He states as he steps out into the bedroom.

I sit there in shock at what has just taken place. No one has ever done anything like that for me before. He was gentle and never touched me in a sexual way, but I have never been more aroused in all my life. My nipples are peaked, and I have already moistened the boxers he placed on me. I am trembling with want and a fluttering in my lower stomach is slowly falling to my sex.

He is back then and sweeps me into his arms gently being mindful of my ribs and carries me to the bed. He lays me down gently and covers my shaking body with the cover. He must think I'm cold from the bath, so I'm not going to tell him any different. He places a hand on my forehead with a concerned frown on his face.

"You don't feel like you have a fever. It's too warm in here for you to be cold." He states. I don't reply. I just snuggle down into the cover and close my eyes. I'm so weak. The shower has completely depleted my strength. He climbs in the other side of the bed and wraps me in his warmth to still my chills. In moments I am asleep and dreaming of the shower all over again.

CHAPTER 6

HAWK

"HAVE we gotten any more intel on the gun runners?" I ask the group of men sitting around Charlotte's room.

"From what we have gathered, the guys we are after have moved out of the area. The place we attempted to raid the other day when we found Charlotte is one of their hideouts, but those men that were holding her are not part of their crew. They were apparently squatting on their property." Wolf, head of the SEAL team informs me.

"How's she doing? Will she be able to travel soon?" Mozart inquires. "We will need to be ready to move once we get word on their location. However, we don't need to risk her life. We can regroup and even have another team come in to take over if we need to extract her out of here."

"She's doing fucking amazing considering her injuries. I know those ribs have to hurt like hell, but she never made a sound when I got her up and made her take a shower." I inform the group. I feel proud of the woman and her strength. "I'm not sure about travel just yet. She was so exhausted from the shower she fell asleep immediately upon hitting the pillow." A chorus of chuckles sounds around the room.

Sitting on the bed next to her I can't keep from running my fingers through her soft hair. Deadeye is sitting in the chair next to her bed while the rest of the men from both teams take up chairs around the room. Charlotte's eyes flutter open and begin to dance around the room, flitting from one alpha male to the next. All of the men on these teams are large, muscle bound men. They are dressed in camo and have weapons strapped to their bodies. They are always alert and ready for anything. It's comforting to know they will help me keep her safe.

"Good afternoon, love. Are you ready to try and eat again?" I question her as all eyes in the room turn to look at her. She looks overwhelmed at all the testosterone radiating around the room. She tries to sit up while keeping the cover over her chest. She is still very weak, so I assist her into a comfortable position on the bed. The t-shirt I put on her is thin and snug over her breasts. We had cut her bra off when we brought her here, so the shirt is almost obscene. I don't want anyone else looking at her.

"Yeah, I'll try." She says looking around at all the men in the room.

"I will get something warmed up." Dude a brown headed man from the SEAL team says. He is near the door and heads out it in a flash.

"We are glad you are awake and seem to be feeling better." Wolf tells her. His concern for her is easy to see. Again, I am thankful to have not only my team, but his as well to help me keep her safe.

"Let me make some introductions." I tell her. "That's Deadeye sitting there next to you. The blonde knuckle head behind him is, Straw. Next to him is Mercury, Wallace, Tank, and Ace. Behind them are Virus, Worm, and Hack. We are Marines Special Ops also known as Raiders. The SEAL team is sitting at the foot of the bed. The older guy that just spoke to you is Wolf. He's their leader. Next to him is Mozart, Abe, Cookie, and Benny. The guy walking in with your food is Dude."

Charlotte quietly surveys the room. Is she uncomfortable with all these men around her? After what she has been through, it might make her afraid. Dude walks up to her and places the tray on her lap. He makes sure everything is open and ready for her to eat. A glass of water is on the tray as well. Charlotte reaches out for it. Her hand trembles violently as she tries to bring it to her lips. I grab the glass from her hand before she can spill it. Lifting the cup to her lips she takes a small sip. All eyes in the room are watching us as I feed her. She looks like she wants to just disappear. She looks up at Dude and whispers her thanks for the food.

"There's no need for thanks, sweetheart. We are just glad you are able to eat something. I wasn't convinced you would pull through the day we found you in the jungle." Dude states frankly. Others verbalize their agreement with grunts. She reaches out to get the fork on the tray, but I swat her hand away and proceed to feed her. The men seem to settle in, content to watch.

"I heard you all discussing the gun runners. I need to tell you what I know about them." Charlotte relays to us between bites as I am feeding her. "I overheard them talking about a big shipment of guns and drugs set to cross the border in Texas. They didn't know I spoke or understood Spanish, so they spoke freely in front of me.

They know the officers, their schedules, and when they change out. They are going to kidnap members of their family and use them to get the officers to let them bring everything across. It's set to happen sometime soon, but I didn't get an exact date. They seemed to be very certain they would be successful."

"When did you hear all this?" Wolf asks.

"I sorry, I'm not sure it's been several days, a week maybe. I had a hard time keeping track of the time."

"That's understandable." Deadeye replies. "How many men were keeping you captive?"

"Most of the time there were only three men, but they had company the day I overhead about the shipment." She shivers as she remembers the men that were there that day. "There were 3 other men there that day. They only stayed a short time. I think that one of my captors, Asshole, was related to one of the other men. The leader of the newcomers called him brother and asked why they were there. Asshole replied that it was a family hideout and he had as much right as anyone."

"Asshole?" Straw inquires as the men all chuckle.

"Yeah, I didn't know their names, so I named them in my head. The other two I named Tweedledee and Tweedledum as they seemed rather simple." Charlotte replied with a slight blush of embarrassment at her explanation.

"Can you describe the men, especially the leader?" I ask. I don't want to upset her, but she may be able to shed some light onto the men we are dealing with.

"He was evil looking. His eyes were black and cold. It was like looking at Satan, himself. He had short black hair and a mustache. He was fairly tall as far as men go. He was fairly slim, but muscular." She shudders again as another memory flashes in her mind.

"What did they do to you?" I ask, but not sure if I can handle what she might revel. She just shakes her head. I place my hand gently on her chin and turn her to look at me. "Tell me love, what has you so rattled and shaking." I softly command her to answer me. She closes her eyes and taking a deep breath relates what happened.

"I was just remembering Asshole offering me to the leader, Satan. Thankfully he had declined saying he didn't have time to fuck a filthy American in a tool shed, but to bring me to him in a few days and he would break me in." Her voice was soft, but everyone heard what she said. My eyes dart to my men and see the same look of revulsion that I feel. Once again, I have an overwhelming urge to hunt those men down and give them a slow painful death at the hands of the best trained soldier America has to offer. I'm not sure how much longer I can keep the anger at bay, but I need to try for her sake.

"Mother fucker!" Cookie exclaims.

"Bastard!" Tank mutters. Several others swore at Charlotte's announcement.

Charlotte clamps her mouth shut as I try to place some of the pasta meal into her mouth. She shakes her head in protest as I try again. It concerns me. She isn't taking in enough to sustain her much less heal her battered and broken body.

"You need to eat to build your strength up." I state firmly, using my Daddy voice that gets Brian to comply with any request.

"I know, but I just can't." She whines. "It's been months since I have had anything remotely decent to eat. I truly appreciate your concern, but I don't want to get sick. I hate throwing up and in the shape I'm in at the moment I don't think I could stand it. God, it would hurt my ribs so bad." She declares with fresh tears in her eyes. She looks up to the twelve pairs of eyes boring into her with concern and empathy. It's all over now. The tears flow freely down her face as a sob escapes her lips.

CHAPTER 7

CHARLOTTE

THE MEN all clear the room as Hawk takes me into his arms again trying to soothe me. I feel like such a child. I need to get it together. The last thing they need is to be worrying about a mess of a woman. But when I saw the concern and empathy from these hardcore badass Alpha males, it was all over. The tears were again flowing freely. Once my tears have abated, Hawk wipes my face gently.

"You ok now, love?"

"Yes, I'm sorry I'm such a mess. I can't seem to stop them once they start." I tell him.

"It's completely reasonable. You have been through a lot over the last few months and you are hurt, in a foreign country, and with a group of strangers. But know this, we will do our very best to get you home to your family and ensure that you are never hurt again." Hawk says with such intensity that I shiver under his stare.

"I know and I am so thankful that God put you on that trail when I needed you so desperately. I don't think...No, I know I would not have survived what they were intending to do to me. I'm not strong. I know that. I would have given up and fallen into the despair they wanted me to so they could control me."

"I know you don't want to relive what happened, but you need to talk about what happened to you. What they did to you. I am here and I will listen all day if you will just talk to me. Get it out. It will make it easier to move on from this nightmare." Hawk tells me as he gently runs his hand up and down my back as I lay my head on his chest. He has his chin resting on top of my head. I decide I need to reassure him that I wasn't raped. I know that's what he is thinking. I take some deep breaths to steady my nerves and begin to tell him about my ordeal over the last few months.

"They beat me daily. They mostly only gave me water but occasionally brought some bread or raw vegetables. They didn't seem to want anything other than to make me hurt at first. The day you found me something had changed though. After Tweedledee had beaten me again, he let me know that things were going to change that day." I say as I settle further into Hawk. Running my hand over his chest to distract me from the awful memories running through my head, I decide I need to get this over with and tell him what had happened that last day.

"After the beating they usually left me alone for the day, but that day he said it was time to teach me how to be a good girl. They were going to give me to Satan, and he wants obedient women. Tweedledee said he was going to show me how be good and do what the man wanted. He said a lot of shit that I won't repeat. I'm sure you can imagine." My voice wavers as the memory vividly plays out in my mind. "He groped me and bit my breasts. He proceeded to remove my pants and underwear… I tried to get away, but my hands and my feet were chained to the floor. I managed to crawl a few feet away, but once he had his pants down, he pulled me back to him." I shudder and my voice hitches as I try to continue to relive the nightmare.

"I'm so sorry, love." Hawks says as he continues to run his hand down my back trying to soothe me. It takes a few moments before I can continue.

"I could feel him at my entrance. He had me from behind and his fingers were digging into my hips. I was so scared. I knew he was going to rape me and there was not a damn thing I could do to stop him. Just when he was about to penetrate me, Tweedledum began shouting outside and jerked to door open to the shed I was in. He ranted in Spanish and the man behind me suddenly jumped up and righted his clothes. He pulled me to my feet by my hair and pulled my pants back up. They secured my hands and feet again with the zip ties, then they drug me out to the jeep and threw me into the back. The whole camp was in chaos. I guess they must have heard or seen you guys coming through the jungle. The rest you know." I finish.

"You weren't raped?" Hawk asks. "I saw the bite marks on your breasts and the bruises on your hips and thighs. I was sure that the worst had happened." His voice is soft and quiet.

"No, I wasn't." I reply. "Thanks to you."

"Thank God!" Hawk declares as he lets out a huff. He had apparently been holding his breath as I related my story. "While they may not have completed the act, you were still violated. I hate that those bastards touched you. I want to kill them all." He seems so sincere. I decide I need to tell him everything.

"You kept me sane." I say as I raise my head and look

into those gorgeous eyes. I go on to explain when he frowns at me in confusion. "Do you remember meeting me in the airport back in San Diego?"

"Yes, how could I forget you? You were so sincere when you came up to us to thank us for doing our job." Hawk says while rubbing his hand over my cheek.

"Well, I remembered that day too. While I was laying in that shed, getting beaten, I let my mind drift to you and your green eyes. I know this will sound crazy, but I felt a connection to you that day when you touched my arm. I would fantasize that you would come find me and save me from the nightmare that had become my life. I kept thinking about how kind you were. I knew that you would help me if you knew what was happening and where I was."

"I would have been here sooner if I had known, love because I felt a connection, too. I've thought about you too since that day." Hawk pauses for a moment, then asks, "Is that all you fantasized about? Me coming to rescue you?" He looks down at me with heat in his eyes. I blush and lower my eyes.

"A girl has to have some secrets." I smile coyly in answer to his question. There is no way I'm about to tell him all the dirty thoughts or the dreams I have had since meeting him in the airport that day.

Hawk chuckles and says, "I'll take that as a No. Good." He shifts me so that I am laying on my back and he is leaning over me.

"Are you ok like this? I don't want to hurt your ribs." Hawks says as he shifts our bodies some more. He frowns down at me in concern.

"I'm ok." I say then laugh. "I'm more than ok like this."

"Good. Tell me about these fantasies. Maybe I can make them come true." Hawk is looking at me so intensely that I can hardly breath. His green eyes are boring into me like he can see into my soul.

"Umm…I think I will let you try to guess what they were." I say breathlessly. He just continues to stare at me with his intense gaze for what seems like forever. Then as if he has made some sort of decision, he nods then closes the distance between us.

He brushes his lips over mine. Gently, testing my reaction. His lips are perfect just as I had dreamed, they would be. His kiss is soft and gentle at first. He pulls back to look at me. I slide my hand behind his neck and pull him down for another kiss. He runs his tongue over my lips, begging for entrance. I part my lips in answer and he devours me. The kiss deepens. He angles my head so he can get the access he wants. Our tongues dance and tease one another. I feel my nipples harden as my breast rub against his chest through the thin fabric of the t-shirt. A moan escapes my lips, but he consumes it with his mouth. My hands have wondered down his broad, firm back. How long we feast on one another I'm not sure as time seemed to stand still. After a long while, but yet still seems too soon, he pulls back to look into my eyes.

"Was I close, love?" Hawk asks with humor in his eyes. He laughs as all I can do is nod at his question. My breathing is a little labored, and goose bumps have formed on my skin. His erection is pressing into sex. I suddenly realize I have opened my legs wide and allowed him to seat himself between them. He moves to get up and I realize he means to call this make out session to an end.

"Wait…um are you going to be alright?" I inquire as he gets off the bed. My gaze has drifted to the bulge in his pants that is easy to see. He adjusts himself, before saying.

"I'll be alright for now, love. You need to rest and heal. I shouldn't have taken things this far. You have been through something horrible and I don't want to make it worse. I'm a patient man. I can wait for my release until I can be inside you. I want to feel your heat and wetness around me as I take you. I want my dick buried in so deep that we are one when I come inside you. I will make more of your dreams come true later, when your ribs are healed. We can't do that right now. It would hurt you, but make no mistake, when you are healed, there is nothing we won't do." Hawk says with determination. I am again blushing like a teenager.

Hours later as I lay in bed alone trying to sleep, my mind replays everything over and over again. He has left to go talk to the others and formulate a plan to get me out of here and back home so I can heal. I wonder, does he really want to be with me? Why would he? I'm no beauty queen. He's seen my stretch marks from carrying my babies, and he doesn't even know me. We don't know anything about each other, he seems sincere though. He's been so kind and concerned for my well being. And Lord! The way he talked to me. No one, not even my husband has ever dirty talked to me like he has. My mind can't seem to think clearly when he is around.

Hawk and the man called Wolf enter my room leaving the light off they take the chairs beside my bed. They must think I am asleep because they continue their conversation in hushed tones.

"Tex says the gun runners have moved their shipment further north about 75 miles from here. He is getting in touch with Commander Hurt to let him know what is going on with the shipment and that we now have a civilian in our care." Wolf informs Hawk.

"I hope for her sake they call us off this mission, so I can get her home. She has been through enough already and I won't risk her getting hurt while we are trying to take out the target. I know my first duty should be to the mission but since she literally fell into my life, she is all I can think about. I find myself putting her first above all else. I have never felt like this about someone before. I've been drawn to her since the first day I saw her. I met her at the airport the day we arrived in San Diego. Did I tell you that?" Hawk says.

"No, I didn't realize you knew her from before." Wolf says.

"Well, I didn't really know her, but she came up to us in the airport to thank us for our service. It was the day we arrived to start this mission. She was so sincere and cute as hell. I couldn't stop thinking about her. I kicked myself for not asking for her number. Then boom there she is laying on the jungle floor tied up, beaten, and unconscious. It's like fate has laid my destiny in my lap. I have to take care of her, make sure she is safe, and that those bastards never hurt her again."

"You want to make her yours, don't you?" Wolf asks with a chuckle.

"Hell, yes she's mine. She just doesn't know it yet. I have hinted at it, but I don't want to push her right now after all she's had to endure in the last 2 months." Hawk declares. "Once I get her back to the States and she's healed though, all bets are off. I will move Heaven and Earth to show her we should be together."

"We have all been there, man. When I met Ice, I knew I couldn't leave her behind. I only hoped she would feel the same about me. Thank God she did, and we have been happily married for a couple of years now. I know how you feel. My guys and I will do all we can to help you take care of her. You know we will. Tex will get the word out and I am sure Commander Hurt will pull us out to get her home for medical treatment. I know you are stationed at Riverton for the foreseeable future, at least until we resolve this Lopez situation. If she is willing to stay in the area, you are welcome to bring her to our house until you can get settled somewhere in a place of your own. We have a small apartment in our basement. I know Ice would be thrilled for you two to stay with us for a while."

"Wolf, I don't know what to say except thanks." Hawk says with a puff of breath. "I really appreciate the offer. I'm not sure what will happen once we are back in the states, but I might take you up on that temporarily. I know I could stay on base, but since we aren't married that would be not be an option for her to stay with me while we are here. Camp Lejeune is our primary base. My son lives nearby with my parents, so once we are done here, we will be headed back to North Carolina."

A knock at the door ends their intense conversation. I am completely freaking out. I am flattered and amazed that he is planning a future with me, but can I leave my little hometown behind to move to another state to live with a man I just met? I'm not sure, but at the same time the thought of leaving him to head home leaves a hollow pit in my stomach. Deadeye and Mozart enter the room.

"Tex has heard back from Commander Hurt. They are going to pull us out. They have another SEAL team on their way to the new location. The helos will be here at 0400 to extract us from the drop site. We need to load up now in order be make it there in time. Commander wanted to pull us out under the cover of darkness. He thinks it will be safer." Mozart informs the men.

"Ok, CSMO and load the Humvees. Once they are loaded, I will get Charlotte up and ready for travel." Hawk says to the men. I hear them agree and the room clears out quickly. I open my eyes and peer around the room. I am alone. It's time to see if I can move around on my own.

I manage to get up and make it to the bathroom. I empty my bladder and wash my face. By the time I make it back in the bedroom, Hawk is there looking perplexed. He sees me wobbling back into the room and hurries to my side and assist me back to the bed.

"What are you doing up by yourself?" Hawk demands harshly. He continues before I even have a chance to respond. "You could have fallen and hurt yourself worse than you already are. What am I going to do with you? Do I need to tie you to the bed? You are going to be the death of me, woman."

"I am fine, Hawk. I'm not an invalid. I know I am weak, but I knew I could do it and I need to get up and move around. You have responsibilities. You can't baby sit me 24/7." I huff. "Besides I heard you guys talking that we will need to leave soon, so I needed to see if I can travel or if you need to leave me here. I won't be responsible for any of you getting hurt or missing your flight out of this awful jungle trying to drag my feeble ass around."

"Hell N!" Hawk growls. "You are not being left behind, no way, no how. I will throw you over my shoulder and haul you out of here if I must. I should turn you over my knee for even suggesting such a foolish thing."

"Hawk listen to me." I say softly as I place my hands

on each side of his face. "I was not a part of your job here. I could not live with myself if you get hurt or God forbid you died, because of me. I won't be the reason any of you don't make it home to your families and friends."

"Charlotte, love, I would not survive if you were left here in this hell hole. I can't explain why or how, but you are under my skin. You are a part of me now. I have to get you home to safety. If you want to keep me safe, you will get your ass out in that Humvee and do every fucking thing I say for you to do. Do you understand?" Hawk demands.

"Ok, Hawk. I will do whatever you say." I whisper. I turn away from him to hide the tears that are welling in my eyes at his harsh words and tone. Slowly, I move to head out of the room.

He grabs my upper arm and spins me around to face him. I keep my head down waiting for him to finish yelling at me and to hide my tears. He places a finger under my chin and forces me to raise my eyes to look at him.

"I didn't mean to be so harsh, but the thought of leaving you here makes me crazy. I shouldn't have yelled at you. I just need you to listen to reason. Just let us get you out of here. Then we can sit down and talk about you and me. Ok? Tell me you feel something between us too?" Hawk asks me.

"Yes, I feel it too. I will do whatever you ask, Hawk." I say as I fall into his arms and rub my hand up and down his back. "I didn't mean to upset you. I'm scared for you, for your men. I'm more afraid of losing you than the men that tortured me for months. I know that sounds insane, but you have touched me, too. I couldn't live knowing that I was responsible for your death."

"No one is going to die, love. I promise you that."

Hawk says. "We are getting out of here, tonight. Come on let's get going."

The trip through the jungle was uneventful. While the rough trail causes me some significant pain, I manage to keep it from Hawk and his men. We reach the extraction point a little early. The men set up a perimeter and wait for the choppers. I have a bad feeling about this. It is just hard for me to believe that after everything that has happened over the last few months, we will just be able to get on a helicopter and fly out of here. I sit quietly while we wait, pondering all that has occurred in the last few days since I have awakened in the care of Hawk. I still can't believe that he plans on us being together once we are back in the States. I want it to be true, but it is too hard for me to wrap my mind around it.

The beating of the choppers as they approach alerts me it's time to go. They are close enough I can smell the fuel from the exhaust. I always hated that smell when we would fly someone out from the hospital, but now it is the smell of salvation. It is so strong it chokes me. We move to run for the ladder, but I trip and fall hard a searing pain runs through my chest, breathing is now very difficult. Hawk sweeps me off my feet and is running for the ladder that has dropped out of the side of the chopper. I didn't want him to send me up first, but I know better than to argue. It will only cost us precious time. I allow him to strap me in and then I am being lifted into the air.

My heart falls out of my chest in fear for Hawk and the other men when I hear gun fire. I stare down at him as he beings to fire his weapon in the direction of the enemy. The ladder sways in the down draft of the chopper blades. I can't keep him in my line of sight. As I swing back where I can see him, he falls backward to the jungle floor. I scream as I am pulled into the side of the helicopter. It takes a sharp turn and begins to pull away from the clearing. I am screaming, fighting against the man trying to hold me back. I have to get to him. They can't just leave him there.

"No, No, No! Go back! You can't leave him there. He's been shot!" I scream at the man holding on to me. He is trying desperately to secure me into a seat and put some headphones on me. I continue to fight him, sobbing and pleading with him to go back and help him. He slips headphones on my head so he can talk to me.

"Ma'am you have to calm down. I don't want to hurt you. I was told you have several broken ribs. Settle down so I can get you strapped into a seat." The man says calmly.

"You will not leave them! I will fucking jump back out of this damn chopper and take you with me, if you don't go back for them right now." I yell at the man. I still haven't allowed him to secure me to the seat. I grip his arm firmly and move toward the open door.

"Alright, alright we will swing back around and try again. Hawk would end me if I let you jump out of the bird. We won't leave them there under enemy fire." The stranger reassures me. I stop struggling and let him place me in the seat belt of the seat. I close my eyes and pray with all my might, that we will be able to get him in this helicopter with me soon. I can't survive this. I can't lose him, now. I feel the aircraft make another sharp turn as we head back to get my saviors.

It seems to take forever after they drop the ladder for me to see his face come into the helicopter. I am out of my seat and clinging to him as soon as he is inside. I am so thankful he's here. I just have to make sure he isn't hurt to badly. I am trying to see where he was shot. I see blood everywhere, but I can't find and entrance or exit wound. He is not cooperating with my efforts to find the wounds. He is saying something, but I can't hear over the noise of the blades and with the headphones on. The stranger puts a pair of them on him and I can finally hear him.

"Love, stop, I'm ok. It's just a flesh wound. You need get back in your seatbelt in case we have to bank. I don't want you falling out." Hawk says in as calm a voice as he can.

"You aren't dying?" I plead with him to reassure me that he is being honest. My eyes search his for the truth. I just knew that it was very bad, and I would watch him die or worse would never lay eyes on him again. "Are you sure it didn't hit a lung or your heart?"

"No, love I'm ok." He chuckles at my medical question. "It got me in the upper right shoulder. It hurts like hell, but it's not bad. Deadeye covered it while we were waiting for you to circle back." I settle back into the seat like he asked. I had promised him after all that I would do whatever he said as long as we all got out of there alive. I see the other team members climbing into the chopper and another one is beside us loading up more of the team.

"Which was not supposed to happen by the way. Who the hell gave you permission to circle back?" Hawk asks the soldier that was helping everyone on board. The soldier just motions over toward me.

"She threated to jump back out and take me with her sir. I couldn't refuse a request like that." He says with a grin. Deadeye begins laughing and gives Hawk a look that says, 'I told you so.'

CHAPTER 8

HAWK

THIS WOMAN CONTINUES to amaze me. She is so physically strong. She fights against the pain of her injuries and tries to hide her emotional pain of the hell she endured. It was all I could do to restrain myself from fucking her. God, her body was so receptive and responsive to my touch. She will be a wildcat in bed when she is healed. I am looking forward to learning all about her then.

She is brave as well. She freely discussed the gun runners plans with us. She didn't seem to be afraid of us even though the room was full of tough, badass military men. After what she endured, she should have been terrified to be in that small room with so many powerful men. Later when I insisted, she tell me what all had been done to her in the time she was held captive, she completely opened up and reveled all. I know it wasn't my place to question her about her torture, but I had to know if she had been raped. I don't think I could sit here knowing that had happened. I would have to hunt those bastards down and make them wish they had never been born.

I can't believe she thought that we would even consider leaving her behind. I appreciate that she is worried for our safety, but she needs to understand we are highly trained professionals. We will get her safely on the chopper and all of us will be going home. There is no need for her to be worried. We always get the job done.

She is the toughest woman I have ever met. I know she's hurting as we bounce through the jungle. I can see the sweat breaking out on her forehead, yet she hasn't made a sound. I reach over to run my fingers through her hair. She smiles at me trying to put on a brave face. I am getting edgy while awaiting the transport out of here. This has to work. I have to get her out of here. Once we get to safety, we can figure this whole thing out.

Gunfire breaks out as Charlotte is being lifted into the helicopter. What if she is hit before she can get into the chopper? I have my Mk 48 up and firing in seconds. A searing pain blasts through my right shoulder as I am thrown backwards hitting the jungle floor. Fuck! I'm hit. Before I have time to assess the damage, Deadeye is hovering over me.

"You ok man?" Deadeye questions me.

"Yeah, I'm hit but it's not bad. Just a flesh wound," He grabs the handle on my gear and begins to drag me into the trees for cover. Once we are secured behind cover, I relate what's on my mind.

"They got her. She's on the way out." I reply as the chopper makes another approach. What the fucking hell? They were supposed to get her out of here, not come back for us. "What the hell are they doing?" I screech to Deadeye. "That's not in the plan."

"I have a feeling your little woman threw a fit until they agreed to come back for you. She saw you go down. I saw her face. It was utter terror." Deadeye smirks me. "You are going to have your work cut out for you with this one. She's trouble with a capital T. Come on let's get you in there before she forces them to land right here."

Once everyone is on board and we are out of danger. I check on the team.

"SITREP" I demand over the mic.

A round of "PFA" resounds in my ear. My team is all on board and no serious harm. It's a good day.

* * *

ONCE THE CHOPPER lands at a secure airport, we disembark and head to a fixed wing that will take us back to the States. It's an Army cargo plane. No comforts of home, but it has enough fuel to take us all the way back to San Diego without having to refuel in Texas. Charlotte has attached herself to me like glue and has followed my every request. I have to admit I am loving it. I didn't want her to be frightened, but if it means she will do what I say so that she is safe. I'm ok with it. Give me a flesh wound any day if it means she is safe and secure.

The SEAL team and my men are all with us and have only suffer minor cuts and bruises. We were damn lucky we didn't lose someone today. I fully realize it could have been me. My right shoulder reminds me with every move I make.

"Here Hawk, let me see how bad that is." Mozart says as he comes up to my chair once we are in the air. Charlotte has already been trying to get a look.

"Let me see it!" Charlotte demands.

"We got this Charlotte. We are combat trained

medics," Straw eases her back as he moves to assess my wound.

"I don't give a rat's ass what kind of damn training you have had. I'm a nurse practitioner with years of Emergency Room experience. I'm going to assess his wound." Anger flares on her face and she pushes back against Straw. Deadeye again gives me the look. I know what he means. I have one feisty woman on my hands. Mozart and Straw assess my wound while I work on distracting Charlotte by stroking her hair and try to maneuver her onto my lap.

"You are an exasperating patient. You won't do anything I say." Charlotte huffs at me, struggling to get a decent breath. "Now stop trying to distract me from taking care of you. I don't know how long it will be before we can get you to the hospital."

"Charlotte, stop fussing. I'm fine. Straw and Mozart know what to do in these situations. They have taken care of more gunshot wounds than you have I'm sure." I scold her. Hurt flashes across her face and she drops into her seat in defeat. "You need to be taking care of yourself. I can see you are in pain and I don't like the way you are breathing."

I motion for Mozart to assess Charlotte. He moves to her side and begins checking vitals. He places oxygen on her and my concern for her increases.

"Charlotte, I'm going to put some oxygen on you. Your O2 sat is quite low and your heart rate is too fast." Mozart informs her. "This should help."

Charlotte's skin is pale, and her breathing is very labored. Her face is drawn and she's staring off into space. Her body slumps as the adrenaline rush leaves her. I reach for her and she allows me to pull her onto my lap for the rest of the flight. Her body sags into mine and she rests her head on my shoulder. I tighten my hold on her. We can't get to base fast enough to suit me. She needs medical attention sooner rather than later.

CHAPTER 9

CHARLOTTE

We are finally in a position to fully assess Hawk's wound. He was right in that it doesn't appear to have hit any major organs, blood vessels, or bones, but he has lost quite a bit of blood. He is the worst patient ever. He won't lay still and let me work. He keeps trying to distract me from caring for him. He insists on sitting up in a chair instead of lying on a stretcher in the back. When he tries to pull me into his lap, I frown down at him. Mozart is suddenly at my side, checking my vitals and placing oxygen on me. It's harder to breathe now and I don't have the strength to fight with them any longer. Giving in I relax on Hawk's lap for the rest of the flight.

When we land at the military airport, there are two large black vans waiting to take us away. I am relieved that word has not leaked out about me being among the soldiers. Wolf had said that if word had leaked out, we would be swarmed by reporters and camera crews wanting a story. He assured me they would do their best to get me away from them and into an awaiting vehicle as quickly as possible. My only concern is to make sure that Hawk is taken to the hospital so he can be treated for his injuries.

The vans take us to the base hospital. Forced to leave Hawk to the care of strangers, they take me to another room and began to assess my injuries. Straw and Ace follow me into the exam room but are sent out of the room because they are not family.

"How's Hawk? The soldier that was shot. I need to know how he's doing." I ask the doctor that comes in to see me.

"Ms. Williams I cannot discuss other patients with you. It's patient confidentiality. You understand." The doctor replies.

"Look you can tell me if he is stable or not. I'm not asking for his medical record. I need to know if he is ok. Just tell me!" I demand.

The doctor and nurses all refuse to tell me anything. It's taking too long for him to come see about me. If it's only a flesh wound, he should have already been released. Deciding to go see for myself what is going on, I take off the oxygen mask and move to get off the stretcher. The nurse reaches out to stop me. I jerk away from her and move toward the other side of the stretcher. The doctor moves to block me as he is calling for security. The heart monitor is alarming, but I don't care. Irrational fear has taken over. Impending doom. Something is wrong and I need to see Hawk. Straw enters the room. He scans the room taking in the scene before him. I am struggling to get out of the grasp of the nurse so I can get off the stretcher to get to Hawk.

"Straw! Help me! They won't tell me anything and they won't let me up." I am screaming by this time. The doctor has fled the room. Good, at least that's one out of my way. Damn this nurse is strong. I again jerk my arm to get away from her as Deadeye enters the room.

"Calm down, Wildcat. You are getting yourself all worked up. The staff is getting concerned because your oxygen levels won't stay up." Deadeye explains. "You need to lay back and cooperate, before they decide to sedate your ass. Hawk is fine. He wants you to relax until he can come over here. He's just in the next room. They are dressing his wound again. He'll be in here in a minute."

I glare at him, trying to decide if he is telling me the truth or just trying to get me to behave. I puff out a deep breath and lay back on the stretcher. Putting my mask back on, I let them poke and prod me, shoot x-rays, and dress my wounds. If it will speed up getting to see Hawk, see for myself that he is ok, I will be the best patient ever. After what seems like an eternity, Hawk comes to my room and sits beside me. He has a bandage on his shoulder, but otherwise appears to be ok.

"I hear you been giving the Hell, love." Hawk chuckles. "You need to behave yourself before they throw you in the brig." My eye widen. Surely, they wouldn't do that would they? He laughs harder at my reaction. I'm glaring at him while he laughs even more when we get company. The other members of both Hawk's team and the SEAL team have also come in to see how we are doing. The doctor follows them into the room and frowns at us.

"Gentlemen, I need to speak with Ms. Williams about her condition and I am sure you are aware I can't do that with all of you in here." The doctor admonishes.

"You can if I say it ok." I interject. "I know all about HIPPA. I give you permission to discuss my medical treatment in front of these men. I would not be here if not for them." The doctor looks taken aback but proceeds to lay it out for me.

"Let me introduce myself. I am Dr. Jacobson. Ms. Williams, you have a several broken ribs on both sides. You also have a partial collapse of the right lung which will require a chest tube to inflate the lung. We need to get that put in as soon as possible. That is why you are unable to maintain your O2 levels without oxygen. You also have a small subacute subdural hematoma. It appears to be resolving, but we need to keep an eye on it. You will need to remain here for the next several days. Do you have any questions?"

"No, let's get this over with. I know it going to hurt like a bitch, so I hope you are generous with the good drugs." I try to smile, but it's most likely a grimace. Hawk squeezes my hand gently. The doctor looks around the room and smiles.

"You have quite the entourage Ms. Williams. I'm afraid however that I can't work with this many people in here. I will have to insist they leave while we get the chest tube in." The doctor motions for the men to leave the room. One by one they come to my bedside and whisper encouraging words before they depart. At last, Hawk is the only one left. I try to put on a brave face for him. I'm scared because I know this is going to suck big time, but I don't really want him to see me wimp out either.

"I'm not leaving Wildcat. I know this is going to hurt and I need to be here for you." Hawk states matter of fact. He moves to the left side of the bed and takes my hand. I want him to be with me more than anything right now. Somehow, I am not as afraid with him here. The doctor looks at us questioningly, once they have everything ready to begin.

"Please, I want him to stay." I tell the doctor. "I promise I will be a much better patient if he is in here than if you make him leave."

"If you insist Ms. Williams. I will warn your boyfriend this is not a pretty procedure." His eyes meet Hawk's. "If you pass out, we won't be taking care of you until we are done with her." Dr Jacobson turns to me and says, "I will make sure you are comfortable. We will give you some pain medication before we start, and I will numb the site."

Dr. Jacobson was true to his word. The nurse brought in a nice little shot of Morphine. Which helped to make me a little loopy, but once he popped the tube through my chest wall, I was wide awake. It was a searing pain in my side. However, it was amazing how quickly my breathing eased off after the tube was in. I hadn't realized how hard it had been to get a good breath. Once they are done and I am taped up nine ways to Sunday I finally relax enough to drift off to sleep.

CHAPTER 10

HAWK

A FEW HOURS later once Charlotte is settled into an ICU room. Commander Hurt, leader of Wolf's SEAL team comes by her room.

"Ms. Williams, I realize you have been through a lot in the last couple of months. I hate to spring this on you right now, but it has to be dealt with sooner rather than later." Commander Hurt says. "I have a couple of favors to ask. Our missions are top secret for the most part. We would like to keep your rescue out the news for the time being. At least until we can finish what we had started there. Also, once this is over, please don't mention the names of the men that helped to bring you home."

"I understand, but what about my family? I need to let my kids know that I am alive. I know they have to be worried." Charlotte replies Commander Hurt.

"We have already sent some soldiers from Fort Campbell to notify your children. We are flying them out here as soon as possible. We have asked them to sign confidentiality agreements to not disclose your return." Commander Hurt informs her. "I would like for you to remain under our care and protection while we complete our mission. Once that is settled, we will make a press release."

"Thank you so much." She answers him. He gives her a long look before continuing.

"The other favor is my SEAL team would like to come by and visit you while you are here. If you are comfortable with that. They would like to be able to tell their wives about you and allow them to visit as well. Wolf tells me he thinks you actually met some of them at a bar here in Riverton, before you left the country on your ill-fated trip." Commander Hurt relays.

"I would be honored for them to visit. I would like to thank them for the sacrifice they make when their husbands are deployed on missions." Charlotte is always thinking of others before herself. Commander Hurt turns his gaze on me. I have been parked in a chair at her bedside all day.

"Hawk your commanding officer will be by later. He asked that I let you know you are on sick leave for the next month while your shoulder wound heals." Commander Hurt says and winks at us. Charlotte looks at me questioningly. "What was that all about?"

"Nothing for you to worry your pretty little head about. You better try to get some sleep. Once those women find out you are here. You will be swarmed with company and sleep will be hard to come by." I stand up and fluff her pillow and tuck her into bed. "Now close your eyes and sleep, woman. I'll be right here." I settle into the chair next to her bed.

"You sure are bossy. You need to lay down and sleep, too." She grumbles at me. "I'll be alright. This is a military hospital for Heaven's sake. It's not like someone will carry me off in here."

"I'm not leaving so stop arguing and sleep." I demand.

"No. You are dead on your feet. If you won't leave for your own quarters, then you will lay down here with me. You were shot for God's sake and lost a lot of blood. You need to rest. I'm worried about you." She whines in an attempt to get me to comply. Not wanting to disappoint her and knowing it's the only way to get her to sleep, I get up and climb in next to her.

"Move over woman. If it's the only way to get you to sleep, then I will lay down." I snuggle her to my chest being careful not to dislodge any of her lines from her body. I know the nurse will have a fit when she comes in, but for the moment I don't care. I am in Heaven as I listen to the rhythmic beating of her heart and realize how close I came to never be able to hear it again.

I am awoken sometime later by the nurse coming in to check on Charlotte's tubing's, dressings, and vital signs. I keep my eyes closed. My head is on her pillow and my right arm is wrapped around her shoulders. Charlotte's head is resting on my chest and her arm is across my waist. Charlotte whispers to the nurse to please let me stay. She promises we won't disturb any of the monitoring or lifesaving equipment. The nurse whispers back, "I have already heard about you. If I want any cooperation from you, I need to let him stay. I guess as long as it gets you to behave yourself, I can let it slide." Charlotte lays head back down on my chest. Soon she is sleeping again.

The next morning the room is in chaos. It is full of Marines, SEALs, and their wives. The men each come near the bed and introduce their wives to Charlotte and I. Wolf comes in first and we meet his wife Caroline. She is warm and sweet. She hugs Charlotte and fawns all over her.

"Charlotte, do you remember meeting me in Riverton a few months ago?" Charlotte nods in agreement. "I'm happy to see you again, but I'm so sorry you were taken and treated so terribly." She has tears in her eyes as she talks with Charlotte. Next is Mozart and Summer come near the bed.

"It's good to see you again, Charlotte." Summer begins. "I'm just so sorry it was like this." Charlotte agrees and returns Summer's hug.

"You are looking much better than the last time I saw you." Mozart smiles down at us.

The other members of the team come in Dude and Cheyenne, Abe and Alabama, and Benny and Jess. Last is Cookie and Fiona.

"Charlotte, I'm so very sorry." Fiona is struggling to hold back her tears. "If you need someone to talk to, please call me. I understand what you are going through better than most." She leans down to put her arms around Charlotte, and I hear her whisper. "Call me anytime, day or night. You will need someone in the days and weeks to come." She pulls back then and joins the others standing around the room.

"Thank you all for coming to visit me." Charlotte tells the room. "I want to thank you ladies for supporting these men in what they do. I have always admired those that serve but did not fully understand the gravity of what they do until I was under their care and protection. They may be the ones to be in service to our country, but you ladies serve in a different manor. You are the glue that keeps everything together while these men are out saving the world. I will never be able to thank you all enough for giving me another chance at life. I surely thought it was over when I was taken, but then my guardian angles came to my rescue when I was in desperate need." Charlotte's voice breaks and tears are welling up in her eyes. So many emotions flash across her face.

Needing to be near her, I get up out of my chair and stand next to the bed. She scoots over so I can sit with her. I am grateful for the visitors, but Charlotte is getting awfully tired. The nurse brings in another dose of pain medication and that's the signal for the room to clear. "I think it's time for Charlotte to get some rest." I inform the room.

Everyone comes to the bed to tell us goodbye and wish Charlotte well. When it's Caroline's turn, she hugs her and leans in to whisper in her ear. "Wolf has already talked to Hawk about this, but when you are discharged you are both welcome to come stay at our house until you figure things out, ok?"

Charlotte looks up at her in surprise, but then a huge smile comes across her face. She nods in agreement. Wolf and Caroline are on our side of making a go of this attraction between us. It's nice to know that others can see what we feel. I'm not sure what will happen over the next few days, but I know we will have the support of some good friends. Charlotte lays back on the bed and smiles at me. I take her hand and hold it until she falls into a deep drug induced slumber.

CHAPTER 11

CHARLOTTE

I WAKE LATER in the day to find my kids sitting at the foot of my bed. I struggle to sit up and Hawk is right there helping me. They are looking at me with concern, but also confusion. Suddenly I am nervous. What will they think about Hawk? I haven't even mentioned trying to date since their dad passed. Will they be ok with this? Sara is the first to react to my being awake. She comes to the opposite side of the bed from where Hawk is standing guard.

"Mom, you had us so worried. I thought you were never coming home," Sara cries as she wraps her arms around me. "You've lost so much weight. I just can't believe this has happened to you. I hate that your first attempt at adventure turned out so badly."

Justin is next up. He stands there stoically waiting for his sister to finish her babbling and crying. When she backs up. He rushes in and hugs me tightly. "Mom! I knew you would make it back someday. I knew you weren't dead even when JoAnn told us we should give up believing you would ever come home. I knew I would feel it in my heart if you were gone, just like with Dad, but I never did." I am sobbing at this point. I hate so much what they have suffered through while I was missing. Hawk gets some tissues and a wet washcloth for me to wash my face. Once he's satisfied that I am not going to fall completely apart, he leans in to whisper in my ear.

"I'm going to take a walk and give you all some time alone. If you need me, the nurse will be able to find me, Ok?" I nod as I am still too choked up to speak. With a kiss to my forehead, he leaves the room. I stare after him for a little too long. I am brought out of my daydream about the wonderful man that has just left the room when Sara shrieks.

"Mom! What is going on here? Who is that man? Why does he seem like he's a little too friendly with my mother who doesn't date? Where did you meet him? How long have you been seeing him? Spill, spill!" Sara is firing off questions faster than I can think of an answer to the one before.

Justin decides to intervene. "What Sara is trying to say is Lucy, you got some splaining to do."

Well it seems they are taking this better than I thought they would. I get them to sit down as I try to catch them up to date on what has happened since I left our little hometown so long ago. I tell them about meeting the soldiers in the airport, then working clinic in the villages, and about the night I was taken. I spare them as many details as I can about my time in captivity. I tell them that under no circumstances are they to talk to the press about my rescue. Lastly, I tell them about Hawk and how he risked his life to get me to the helicopter so I could come home to them.

"Mom, I don't quite understand. If he was shot, why

is he up roaming around and you are the patient in the hospital. Were you shot too, and you just didn't want to tell us?" Justin asks. He has taken Hawk's chair beside my bed, while Sara sits on the bed next to me. They are both looking at me with confusion and concern on their faces.

"No, I wasn't shot. I suffered some broken ribs that resulted in a partial collapsed lung, but I am going to be fine. The chest tube has caused my lung to inflate and I am sure they will be removing the chest tube later today or first thing tomorrow. I just needed some fluids and antibiotics. It was not the most sanitary of conditions down there." I tell them in an effort to reassure them.

"So, what gives with Mr. Hottie?" Sara demands with a smirk.

"Sara LeeAnn Williams! I'm not sure I know what you are talking about young lady, but I don't appreciate your tone." I joke. I know exactly what she is talking about. I have not so much as looked at a single man in the last five years. They have just witnessed what I am sure they perceive as very intimate contact between their mother and a complete stranger. I know I need to discuss it with them, but I'm not even sure what is going on at this point myself.

"Alright Mom, if you want to keep whatever you are doing with Mr. Secret Hottie Pants a secret that's fine, but don't expect me to spill on my love life either then. That goes for you too right Justin?" Sara declares with finality.

"Oh, I'm with Sara on this one Mom. There is positively something going on between you and what did you call him, Mr. Secret Hot Pants?" Justin looks at Sara. "But if you insist on keeping secrets from your own children, then we are forced to keep ours, too." Justin nods in agreement with his sister. I huff out a laugh, that makes my sides scream in pain.

"Ok, ok stop. You two are ganging up on me. I am not sure what if anything is going on," I answer as honestly as I can. "I need some moral support. I will introduce you to him."

The nurse comes in about that time to change my IV fluid bag. I ask her if she can find Hawk for me. She just smiles sheepishly and says of course she can. It is barely a minute after she has left the room that he is back. He looks from me to the kids and back again with concern in his eyes. I guess he is looking for signs that they are upset with us. I reach for him and he immediately comes to my side, stepping over Justin in the process. I suppress a giggle. It just hurts too much to laugh.

"Hawk, I would like you to meet my children. Sara, she's the oldest and this is Justin my son. Guys this is Staff Sargant Jordon Jackson aka Hawk. He is a Marine and one of the men who helped to save my life and bring me home to you." I take a deep breath, squeeze his hand, and look him in the eyes as I continue. "They want to know what is going on between us." Before either of us can say anything else, Justin speaks up.

"What are your intentions toward our mother? She hasn't dated anyone since Dad died. We would like to see her happy and not be alone, but I won't tolerate anyone, badass Marine or not, using her," Justin declares with venom as he glares at Hawk.

"Michael Justin Williams! Don't you use that tone, young man! I can still turn you over my knee and teach you some manors," I admonish.

"I wasn't talking to you, Mom." Justin replies as he glances at me then turns his eyes back to Hawk. Before I can say anything else. Hawk reaches over and squeezes my hand in reassurance.

"It's ok, love. He is looking out for you and I admire that he is determined to look out for your best interest, just as I intend to do." Hawk says to me as he stares Justin down. "I admire and have strong feelings for your mother. I will do all I can to protect her and keep her safe. I would never intentionally hurt her. I know you don't know me, but I hope you will keep an open mind and let me prove myself to you and your mother."

"Good answer." Justin says as he reaches out to shake Hawk's hand.

The kids only stay for a couple of hours since they had a long flight out and came straight to the hospital. Captain Mark Olson, the man in charge of Hawk's team, comes by to meet me and make arrangements for my family to be put up in a hotel while they are visiting. He informs Hawk, he will need to come in for debriefing tomorrow. By the time everyone has cleared out I am exhausted and just want to sleep.

Hawk takes up guard duty at my bedside. The night-shift nurse was kind enough to let him sleep with me, but before the dayshift arrived, she brought in a recliner chair, pillow, and blanket. She informed us that not all the staff would be understanding. She didn't want Hawk to get kicked out, because she knew he was helping to keep me sane. I had awoken several times in the night with nightmares despite the pain medication. The nurse, Beth, had come running into the room several times to check on me. She told us that my vital signs at spiked suddenly and she was concerned something was wrong internally. I assured her I had only had a bad dream.

"You need anything, love." Hawk asks as I snuggle down to sleep.

"No. I'm fine." I reply. I'm so tired. I am praying that I can sleep well tonight. I watch as Hawk settles into the recliner and closes his eyes. I know he must be worn out as well. I was able to get the day nurse to change the dressing on his shoulder today. She assured me that it was healing fine without signs of infection. I close my eyes and sleep over comes me.

CHAPTER 12

HAWK

I CLOSE my eyes to sleep. It has been a long day. It was nice to meet Charlotte's children. A smile crosses my face when I think about how fiercely her son questioned me about my intentions. I am glad to see he is protective of his mother, but even happier that her children were not upset that Charlotte and I seem to have something between us. When they first arrived, I was concerned they would give her a hard time. Some kids never want their parents to find love after divorce or the death of a spouse. I wasn't sure what kind of reaction they would have, so I am pleased that while they are skeptical of me, they don't seem to be angry about it. It would devastate Charlotte if she thought it was causing her children discomfort. Without a doubt she would put them first and there would be no chance for us. It's time to put these thoughts out of my head and sleep before the nightmares begin.

Charlotte screaming, NO! over and over, startles me from sleep. She is thrashing violently in the bed and I am afraid she is going to hurt herself. I jump into action as the nurse bursts through the door. The bright light of the hallway floods the room and it blinds me. Charlotte screams louder trying to climb up the head of the bed. As I reach for her, I try talking her down from whatever horrors she is seeing in her mind's eye.

"Charlotte! Charlotte! Look at me, love." I admonish her with a firm, but gentle tone. "You are safe, in the hospital on base. It's me Hawk. I am here with you. No one is going to hurt you." I have gotten her attention, but she still looks disoriented. She is frowning at me, but at least she is not pulling away from my hand on her arm.

"They have me tied down and they are going to hurt me." She whispers as tears begin to fall. Her eyes dart around the room wildly as if she is looking for her captors.

"No, love. I am here. I won't let them hurt you. Remember, I promised." I reply in the calmest of tones. It infuriates me that she is having to relive this shit over and over every night. "Come, let me hold you so you can go back to sleep."

"You're really here?" She whispers again. "I'm not dreaming about you?"

"No, love, you are not dreaming. I am right here. See, feel my hand on your arm?" I attempt to pull her back down into the bed. This time she lets me. I sit on the bed with her and pull her to me like we slept in the safe house. Slowly, she relaxes into my chest and runs her hand over it. She whispers to herself.

"He's really here. I am ok now. He's real. I can feel him." She continues to assure herself for several minutes while the nurse checks everything out. It's a miracle she hasn't dislodged some of the tubes they have attached to her, but the nurse says everything is ok. She doesn't seem to mind that I am in the hospital bed with her, so I remain there while she drifts back to sleep.

A couple of hours later I am awoken again to her cries. She calms a little quicker this time. Thankfully, I am able to help her calm down. A couple of times, I am sure she is having a flash back, because even once she seems to be awake, she still looks confused and shaken. By 5 am, we have been up and down several times. She is reluctant to even try to sleep now. So, at her insistence I head downstairs to get her some coffee with her favorite creamer.

When I return with our coffee, the nurse is in the room again. She explains that she came to check the heart monitor because it was not picking up a signal. She had found Charlotte in the floor beside the bed. The nurse assured me that nothing was broken or dislodged when she had fallen out the of bed. The nurse asks if it is ok to put the bedrail up on that side of the bed, so it doesn't happen again. Charlotte's eyes are darting around, not really focusing on anything.

"Charlotte, are you alright?" I ask lifting her chin up so she has to look at me. She frowns at first, but then relaxes and says, "I just got too close to the edge, I guess. I'm just clumsy." She reaches for the coffee and begins to sip it. She won't look me in the eye. An uneasy feeling comes over me. I will need to speak with the doctor this morning and ask for Charlotte to see the psych doctor again today. She is going to need more intense treatment than we originally thought. She has tried to hide how badly this has affected her. She is a strong woman, but no one can endure all that she has and not come out of it a little scarred. She needs to open up about what is happening so we can help her move on from this nightmare.

Charlotte is sleeping finally. The nurse gave her something to help her rest. She looks so peaceful, like an angel. When Dr. Jacobson comes by, I ask him not to wake her. I tell him about the nightmares and that I think she might be having flash backs as at times she doesn't seem to be in the moment. Dr. Jacobson assures me that he will have the psychiatrist, Dr. Hancock come by again today. He gives me some good news, though. The chest tube can come out today. It's progress toward getting her out of here and moving forward. I am thankful she is improving physically, but I am very concerned about her mental health.

* * *

A WEEK LATER...

Charlotte is being discharged today. She has improved every day. She continues to amaze me. She pushes through the pain without complaint. I know she wants out of here so badly. Her children left to go back home yesterday. They were reluctant to leave, but Charlotte assured them she didn't want them to put their lives on hold. It also helped that we promised to come out, once she is able to fly.

The relationship between mother and children is so similar to the relationship I have had with my own parents. It is comforting to me and lets me see a future with her. I know that my son, Brian is going to love her. She is a wonderful mother to her children. They may be grown, but she is still their mother. She commands respect from them but gives it in return. She doesn't belittle them or scoff at their youth when they made some rather immature comments about the budding relationship between us. She is patient, kind, and loving, but firm when she needs to be. It is my sincere desire to head back to the East coast sooner rather than later so I can introduce her to my family. My parents, son, and siblings have been pestering me to send them pictures or Facetime with them so they can meet her. I don't want to rush her. Even though I have met her children, that's a little different. She was hurt and needed her children to know that she is alive and well. And there was absolutely no way I was going to stay away from her for a week.

Some asshole has leaked her rescue to the press and that she is at this Naval hospital. It has been difficult to keep the reporters away. Some high-ranking Navy officer has decided that Charlotte's rescue would make a great story and improve the public's perception of the military. So, she is being required to make a statement to the press which has really pissed me off. I made it clear to Captain Olson and Commander Hurt that she will read a prepared statement but will not answer any questions. They assured me that we will get her away from the cameras as quickly as possible. Some of those asshole reporters have no manors whatsoever. It's shameful the questions they will shout out. Do they seriously think she is going to confess to being raped at a press conference in front of a room full of strangers?

In addition to the press, we also have to worry about Hugo Lopez. Intel indicates that he knows Charlotte may have sensitive information. He has gang members all over the US. Word is out for them to be on the lookout for the American woman, short with brown curly hair, that was rescued by US military. The news has now made her a target of every street thug in the US. All looking to catch some fame and glory by being the one that brings her to Lopez. It will be harder than ever to keep her safe now that her name and face are a national news story.

Commander Hurt and Captain Olson have arranged for me to keep Charlotte with me on base. They convinced the upper brass that her safety was of National Security importance. The intel she has on the Lopez brothers has helped to secure her protection. We had a meeting with both leaders, my team, and the SEALs we were partnered with. Wolf's offer to allow us to stay with him and his wife was considered, but I don't want to risk their safety. As a group we decided that staying on base would be the most secure. It would keep the press away while we recover. Dr. Hancock the psychiatrist will be close also. And while I hate to admit it, I think we will be needing her more than we could ever have imagined. Charlotte's nightmares have continued, and she seems to be worsening each day. I know the lack of good sleep isn't helping. I'm at a loss as to how to help her. I will do everything in my power to get her though this. She is tough as anyone I've ever met and I know if anyone can get past what she has endured, it's Charlotte.

CHAPTER 13

CHARLOTTE

After a week in the hospital, I am finally allowed to leave with a semi clean bill of health. I have follow-up appointments with a pulmonologist and a psychiatrist to ensure that I am handling all of this okay. I give a short statement to the press the morning of my release and then I am whisked away from the hospital out a back door and into an SUV belonging to one of the SEAL team members. The press has been hounding me for interviews since news of my return to the States was leaked to the press, by an unknown source.

I had thought we were going to Wolf and Caroline's house to stay a few days. However, Hawk, Commander Hurt, and Captain Olson have decided it is too risky to stay there or check into a hotel, even temporarily. They are concerned the press might find out and camp outside to get pictures of us or secure an interview. So, we are going to stay in a house on base. I was sure the military would not let me stay on base as I am not one of them and we aren't married. Hawk assured me that my safety while I recover is a priority to his Captain and Commander Hurt.

After arriving on base, we pull up onto a street with houses on both sides of the street. They are all the same, tan siding, a small window to the left of a plain brown door, with a larger picture window on the right side of the door. We stop in front of one of the units. There are a couple of cars in the driveway and a few more on the street. The others file out and I notice they are surveying the neighborhood just as they had done while we were in the jungle. I suppose it so ingrained in them they don't realize they are doing it. Hawk takes my hand and squeezes gently.

"Are you ready, love?" He asks. "I should have warned you. The SEALs wives have insisted on getting the house ready for us. According to Wolf, they will have gone way overboard, and they will want to spoil us some before they leave. I will try to not let them wear you out too much, but they have been so helpful. I didn't want to say no."

"Oh, Hawk. That is so sweet of them. I don't mind having some company for a while. If they wear me out, perhaps I won't wake you up tonight with my nightmares." I tell him with a smile to lighten the mood.

"Ok" he says with a tender look, "Let's do this." He places my hand on my lap and gets out of the SUV. He walks around to my side and opens the door. I scoot to the edge of the seat and prepare to step out. Before I can sit my feet on the running boards, Hawk has slipped his arms under me. His left arm is behind my shoulders and his right is under my knees. He sweeps me out of the truck as I let out a squeal of surprise. He proceeds to carry me to the front door. The men that have accompanied us on the trip here fall in behind us. I slap at his arms with futility and insist I can walk.

He just smirks at me. "Why walk when you can ride?"

As we approach the door, it flies open and I see Caroline waiting for us to enter. As we enter the house, I can hardly see what it looks like for all the people standing around waiting for us to arrive. Hawk's men, the SEALs, their wives, and many people I haven't met before are all standing there smiling at us. The crowd parts as Hawk carries me through the living room. He still refuses to let me walk. The walls are plain white drywall, but I notice a few framed pictures are hanging on the walls. It was hard to see much of the living room furniture, but it looks like a light brown couch, matching love seat, and small coffee table fill the room. There is a massive flat screen television on the far wall. We turn left to leave the living area and enter the next room where, there is a small oak dining table with four chairs in a little nook. The sliding glass door behind the table allows the sun to filter in and light up the space. There is a small kitchen to the right of the nook. It has a large black refrigerator, with matching stove and a microwave tucked under the upper cabinets. The countertops are white tile with a black back splash. The sink is against the back side of the house with a small window above it. White curtains with black checks are hanging at the window.

Hawk again turns left and heads down a short hallway to enter a door at the end on the right. We enter a large master bedroom. It has a huge cherry king size sleigh bed that dominates the room. The bed is covered with a fluffy hunter green comforter. A matching cherry dresser with mirror covers most of the wall at the foot of the bed. A 6-drawer cherry chest of drawers is on the wall with the door. A small nightstand sits on each side of the bed. On the back wall to the right of the bed is an open door that leads to the in-suite bathroom. Another door beside the dresser is closed and I assume it is the closet.

As Hawk carries me toward the bed, Caroline hurries around us and pulls the covers back on the far side of the bed. The sheets are white with small pink flowers and green vines that match the comforter. Hawk gently places me on the bed and covers my legs. The sheets are so soft, and the mattress is just right. There are big fluffy pillows across the head of the bed. Sighing contentedly, I sink down in the covers.

"I want you to rest a little while before we entertain company. The press conference was almost too much for you this morning. Take a nap and when the food is ready, I will wake you for lunch," Hawk commands. I want to protest. It seems rude to sleep when there are so many people out there, but I can already feel my eyes closing. I just nod my head in agreement and sink further into the mattress. I don't even here the door close has Hawk and Caroline leave the room.

CHAPTER 14

HAWK

SHE IS EXHAUSTED. Please let her sleep without waking up crying and afraid. I walk out to thank everyone for coming and see if they need help with the BBQ, but I won't stay long. I am afraid to leave her sleeping by herself. You never know how long she will be able to sleep.

"Thanks everyone for coming to welcome us home. I hope you all don't mind, but Charlotte needs to rest for a little bit before meeting everyone again," I inform the crowd of men and women waiting in the living area.

"Don't worry about anything. Benny, Ace, and I are manning the grill. The girls have all the sides and desserts prepared. Go rest with her. I'll come get you in a couple of hours when the food is ready, and beers are cold." Wolf informs me. I nod and smile at the room as I turn to head back to my Charlotte.

Cookie stops me as I enter the hallway. "How's she doing?" he inquires with concern.

"She's holding up as well as can be expected. She's suffered a lot, but she's a strong determined woman. She will be fine." I say with as much confidence as I can muster.

"I don't want to push, but my Fiona went through something similar and I thought she was handling it too, but I was wrong and missed the warning signs. She had a flash back and took off on us, while I was gone on a mission. It took several days to find her and bring her home. I just want you to know that if you need any help, Fiona and I are here for you both. We have been there and know how hard it can be to make it from one day to the next. Fiona still has bad days and it's been over 2 years since she was rescued. Make her go see Dr Hancock, try to get her to talk to you about how she feels and what she is experiencing. And know that we are here if you need help. All of the guys would come at the drop of a hat if you need help." Cookie put his hand on my shoulder and gives it a gentle squeeze. Deadeye, Straw, Abe and Dude have walked over to join the conversation while Cookie is talking.

"Thanks, I am worried about her." I reply honestly. "She has these nightmares that wake her several times a night. Sometimes, I don't think she is back in reality for a long while afterward. I don't know if it's flashbacks or what, but I have a strong suspicion that she is trying to keep how mentally unstable she is from me. Hell, even from the doctors."

"This may sound a little off the wall and even seem creepy to you, but I recommend having trackers put on her." Cookie states as a matter of fact.

"Trackers?" I question with one eyebrow raised.

"Yes, all our women have them. They chose to wear them. When Fiona disappeared, we were desperate to find her. If she hadn't had my credit card to use, we might never have found her. The others have had situations where they were kidnapped by really bad people. The trackers have saved their lives and even ours." Cookie declares passionately. "Look just think about it, talk to her about it. Tex, monitors the trackers and if something goes wrong, he calls us and let us know where our women are at. We even wear them while on missions. They have GPS in them. If the worst-case scenario happens, we can be tracked and found anywhere in the world."

"It gives us and our women peace of mind. If she should ever have an episode like Fiona and takes off, you will be glad to have them." Abe declares while slapping me on the back in a friendly gesture.

"It's a good idea, Hawk." Deadeye tells me. "After all the episodes you have described in the hospital. I think it would be foolish not to put some on her. It's only a matter of time, before she cracks." Deadeye throws his hands up in a shrug as I start to argue. "I don't mean that in a bad way. I know she is tough as nails. If she weren't, she would have cracked before we found her in the jungle, but what she suffered would make a hardened soldier like us struggle. It's only natural for her to have some PTSD and anxiety. I say plan for the worst and hope for the best."

"Ok, thanks guys. I will talk to her about it. I need to get back there before she has an episode. It's easier to bring her back to reality if I can intervene before she's too involved with the dream." I turn and head down the hall, determined to do my best to care for this woman that has stolen my heart in a few short days.

CHAPTER 15

CHARLOTTE

The sound of knocking on a door awakens me. Hawk's muscular, warm arms that I crave are wrapped around me. Gently scooting away from him, I try to slip out so I can answer the knocking, but Hawk pulls me back against him, shushing me, whispering words of comfort to assure me that I am ok, and no one is going to hurt me ever again. I sigh deeply. I hate that it's the first thing on his mind, that I am having a nightmare again. Twisting around in his arms to face him, I run my hands through his hair. His eyes pop open and I smile at him. He can always take my breath away with his beautiful green eyes. He smiles back and leans in to place a soft kiss on my lips. I want to deepen it and get lost in his touch, but there is again a knock at the door. Hawk startles and pulls back to get out of bed. He crosses over to the door and swings it open.

"Hey, sorry to wake you, but the food is ready, and I didn't want it to get cold," Wolf is standing in the doorway peering in at me.

"Thanks, we'll be out in a few minutes," Hawk replies

softly. Wolf nods once and turns to walk back down the hall. Hawk quietly shuts the door and strolls back over to our bed and climbs in next to me. I sigh contentedly and snuggle into his chest. He runs his fingers through my hair, then lets his hand slide slowly down my back to finally settle on my butt cheek. He gives it a little squeeze.

"Time to get up, love. The guys have barbequed, and the food is done. You need to eat some lunch. You hardly touched your breakfast at the hospital." Hawk continues to rub his free hand soothingly down my body as he talks. "You lost even more weight while you were in the hospital. You need to eat so you can get your strength back."

"Hawk, I may have lost weight, but it's not going to hurt me to lose a few more pounds. Besides, I eat what I can hold. It's going to take a while for me to get used to eating good food again." I huff out a breath in frustration. I know he means well, but my weight loss is the least of my worries at the moment.

"Hey, I like your curves. I don't want you losing any more weight. Plus, you need calories to heal your broken bones, cuts, and bruises." Hawk says as we sit up. He helps me out of the bed and leads me to the bathroom. Once he is sure I am going to be ok, he steps out and pulls the door almost closed. I want to be offended, but he has bathed me more than once so what if I'm using the facilities while he's listening at the door? It's because he is concerned for me. He cares. I can handle that any day.

After I finish in the bathroom, I wait for Hawk to do his business. Once that is over, we head out into the fray that is transpiring in the living room of our small house. The dining table is loaded with dishes of food.

Hamburgers, hot dogs, steaks, grilled chicken breasts, and pork chops fill several large platters. There are bowls of macaroni 'n cheese, Cole slaw, and potato salad. Chips, dips, fruit, and vegetable trays are lining the small bar between the kitchen and dining area. There is enough food to feed a small army.

A chuckle escapes my lips as that thought crosses my mind. We have a small army here, what with the SEALs, the Marines Special Ops, and other support staff that have converged on our tiny abode for the BBQ. Hawk looks over at me with concern, but quickly grins as he deduces my musings. It's hard to believe that I am here, surrounded by the men (and their women) who saved me from certain death. The best part is the handsome man that is looking at me with such deep affection, it takes my breath away. Hawk begins to fill a plate with a little bit of everything. Once it's almost too full to carry, he takes my hand and leads me into the living room. He sits down in a beautiful, fluffy, hunter green recliner. After placing the plate on the coffee table, he reaches for me and settles me into his lap with my legs draped over the side of the chair. He gets the plate of food and begins to feed me like I am a small child. I want to protest, but I have come to learn that once he has it in his head to feed me, there's nothing I can do, but comply.

Hours later the house is, finally, quiet. All the guests have gone home, and we are left alone in our new abode. Hawk seems happy that we have some time to ourselves. I'm still not sure where we stand, but perhaps this will give us some time to get to know one another better.

I should be embarrassed to be shacking up with a stranger, but I am having more trouble handling all of this than I want to admit. Especially at night, I don't want to be alone, because I am plagued nightly reliving the horrors I endured. I am jerked awake several times a night as I feel the boot kicking my ribs, fists hitting my face, and rough hands forcing my hips up to meet his erection. I try not to wake Hawk, but sometimes it is unavoidable as I am screaming and fighting him violently.

I am having flash backs as well, but I have hidden that from everyone so far. At least, I think I have. They started while I was in the hospital. It was late at night. Hawk had gone down to the cafeteria to get some coffee for us. I had had a particularly bad nightmare. It had taken him a couple of minutes to get me to realize it was only a dream. Once he was sure I was at myself and going to be ok, he agreed to get us some coffee and a snack.

Alone in my room it was dark save for the faint light of the monitor and IV pump. Suddenly, I was blinded by a bright light and male voices are speaking Spanish. They are here for me! How did they find me in a military hospital? Instinctively I roll out of the bed to the floor and try to crawl behind the head of the bed, but I am still tied up. Did I dream about the rescue, seeing my family, Hawk? I can't get my arms free to crawl and something is caught on my right side. It hurts as I try to pull it free from my body. It takes several minutes before I realize the room is once again dark and the voices are gone. They have left. They didn't hit me this time.

The light blinds me again before a shadow blocks some of the light from my eyes. Suddenly a woman is at my bedside. She is about my height with short brown hair and she is wearing light blue scrubs. How is she here in the shed? Why aren't her clothes filthy? I look down at myself and see that I am in a clean looking hospital gown. What is happening? Looking around the room, there is a bedside table and the wheels of the hospital bed. I can't reconcile my surroundings with where I am. I look up at the woman in confusion. She looks at me with concern and reaches out to touch me. I flinch and pull back from her.

"How did you end up in the floor?" She asks me. "Did you fall? Are you hurt anywhere?"

When I don't answer, just peer at her in confusion, she takes my hand and says, "You need to get back in bed, Ms. Williams. I need to make sure you haven't pulled your IV or chest tube out. I came in to check your monitor leads. I think one of the has come off, because it is no longer picking up out at the station." She helps me back into my bed and is replacing a patch on my chest while she is talking to me in the most soothing tone. She continues her assessment, checking my IV, Chest tube dressing, and moving on to the equipment sitting around my bed.

Hawk returns a few minutes later. The nurse smiles at him and tells him that I have fallen out of bed while he was gone, but that nothing seems to be disturbed or injured by the fall. He looks at me with concern and questions me about what happened. I am back to myself and I try to think up an excuse. I don't want him to know that I was having an awake nightmare. Where there even Spanish speaking men in my room? Was I hallucinating the whole thing? I can't let anyone know. They will surely think I am losing my mind and move me to the psych ward.

"I just got too close to the edge, I guess. I'm just clumsy." I lie as I look down at my hands. I take the coffee and sip its warmth. I feel guilty for lying, but I can't take the chance that I'll be locked up in here. If I can just get away from all this I can get back to normal.

Well now that we are out of the hospital, I am hoping the nightmares will stop. Once Hawk has made sure the house is locked up after everyone has left, we head to the bedroom. We take turns in the bathroom getting ready for bed. He hovers outside the door while I am brushing my teeth. I am much stronger now. It is still painful to cough and deep breath, but I am moving around much better. I come out the bathroom and dressed in a night shirt that hits about mid-thigh. I climb into the bed and sink down into the covers to wait for him.

A few minutes later, Hawk emerges from the bathroom in a pair of sleeping pants and no shirt. His muscles ripple as he moves across the room. It's a sin for anyone to look so good. I'm suddenly nervous. We are completely alone. We have shared a bed for almost 2 weeks now, but always knowing we were not really alone. In the jungle the other men were there. At the hospital, a nurse or doctor could enter the room at any time. Now, it's just the two of us.

Hawk walks around the bed to the side closest to the door. He pulls the covers back and lays down on his back. After a few minutes, he turns on his side to face me. He is so close I can feel his breath on my face. My body quivers in anticipation. Will he want to simply sleep? Or will he want to take what we started in the jungle further. I know it's too soon, but I am hoping for the later. I need him, more than I thought would be possible.

"I want you to be comfortable Charlotte. Are you alright with me sleeping here with you? I know we have shared a bed before, but that was different. We always had other people around. I can sleep in the guest room or on the couch, if you aren't comfortable with this." Hawk speaks softly.

My heart is full to bursting. He is worried about how I feel about being alone with him. He would give up his comfort for me. I reach out my left hand and place it on the right side of his face. I smile reassuringly at him.

"Thank you for thinking of my comfort above yours. If you want to sleep in the bed next to me, that is exactly where I want you to be. I am more than comfortable with us sharing a bed. I trust you completely. I know we are technically strangers, but still I know you will not hurt me or force anything on me that I am not ready for," I sigh and scoot closer to him. "Hawk we are not kids; we are adults. We have seen and done enough that we can know what we want. Because we are older, we realize that we don't have unlimited time. Life is short and it can be gone in the blink of an eye. I learned that firsthand when my husband left this world unexpectedly. After the summer I have had, I will no longer spend time worrying if I should do something or what others think about what I am doing. If it's something I want, I am going to go for it. If I wait, it could be gone forever."

CHAPTER 16

HAWK

"Come here, love." I demand reaching for her, pulling her close. She snuggles into my embrace. Taking her chin in my hand, I lift it, so she is forced to look at me. I can't keep the smile from my face as I move in to devour her. I meant to keep is sweet and tender, but once I get a taste of her, I can't stop myself. The kiss is hard, urgent, and demanding. Pushing my tongue into her mouth she meets me with the same desire. Our tongues dance and duel in a fierce battle. My hand moves of its own accord and cups her breast through her night shirt. Her thin shirt is sliding up her thighs giving me a peak at what lies beneath. My knee instinctively slides between her warm, thick thighs.

She moans as I rub my thigh against her sex. So far she isn't showing any signs of fear at what we are doing. She is wet and warm against my leg. It takes all my will power to not slide my pants down and sink into her hot folds. I need more of her. Reluctantly I leave her lips and move my lips down her jaw and neck. As I nip, suck, and lick my way down her neck, she arches her neck to give me better access. Her hands move up and down my back. It encourages me to continue and give her more. Pinching her left nipple between my thumb and index finger, I roll it gently then tug on it. Her nipple is hard under my touch, so I lower my head and take it all into my mouth through her shirt. I'm gentle as I don't want to bring on a flashback. I want the material out of my way, but this is so erotic. She arches eagerly into my mouth. Her hands slide down my back and she squeezes my ass and pulls me into her. My erection is pressing into her moist heat. A growl escapes my throat before I can suppress it. I am about to rip our clothes from our bodies and take her hard and fast when I hear her giggle. Her melodious sound brings me back to reality.

Pulling back, I realize we are both panting like we have run a marathon. Her lips are swollen from our fierce kissing. She has somehow come to be under me, and I shift so my weight is not pressing into her. Her eyes are dilated and full of desire. She is still breathing hard and her hot wet sex seems to be throbbing against my thigh. I want to take her so badly, but I sense a hint of uncertainty. I want there to be no doubt in her eyes when I take her.

"God, you undo me woman. I want to take you, fuck you hard until you are screaming my name with your release. But I don't want to rush this, to rush us. You are not healed, physically or mentally. I am going to turn you around and hold you next to me. And we are going to sleep, for now. But be warned, soon, very soon, we are going to finish this." I inform her as I ease her onto her side and pull her back to my front. My left arm slides under her neck to cradle her head on my shoulder. Draping my right arm across her body my hand finds comfort in cupping her large ample breast. My erection throbs against her backside. How am I ever going to be able to sleep with her hot ass on my dick. I lay awake listening to her breathing as it slows, becoming even and regular as sleep overtakes her.

* * *

THE NEXT WEEK passes without incident. We fall into a sort of routine. We wake early and fix breakfast together. We spend our mornings talking, getting to know each other better. She loves music, all kinds which is something we have in common. She also loves to sing, but insists she sounds terrible. I disagree. Her voice is beautiful. I love hearing her singing with the radio while cooking in the kitchen. She can belt out a country tune or get down with a good ole rock 'n roll classic. Sometimes, I join in and sing with her.

We don't always agree on movies. She prefers the sappy love stories while I prefer more action adventure type movies. We both love comedies and mysteries which makes picking a movie a little easier. Neither of us likes horror movies. She commented that I probably seen enough horrors while in combat and she had while working in a hospital that we didn't need to watch movies about it.

I take Charlotte to see Dr Hancock each day at one in the afternoon. She is uncomfortable talking about her experiences. She fidgets, doesn't make eye contact, and sighs frequently. Sometimes I sit in on her sessions and others I wait outside while she talks with the doctor. The need to take this away from her is overwhelming, but I can't change what has happened to her.

After her appointment, we go by headquarters and meet with the men on both teams and our superiors. Bits and pieces of information come to Charlotte during her sessions with Dr Hancock, so we make sure to update them after each appointment. By the time those meetings are over, it's time for the evening meal. We have picked up take out several times and we have cooked together a few times. Wolf and Caroline invited us over for supper tonight, but Charlotte just couldn't do it. The lack of sleep is catching up with her. As soon as we came home today, she went straight to bed without even eating.

She isn't getting much better. Dr Hancock discussed starting some medications today, but Charlotte refused. She said, "It's too soon to resort to medications. I don't want to be drugged to forget what happened. I need to learn to deal with it and I will in time. I'm not saying that at some point I might need an antidepressant, but I want to give myself more time to heal naturally." Dr. Hancock agreed to give her a couple more weeks before starting medications.

Physically she is getting stronger every day. She refuses to take the pain pills more than once a day and only then so she can try to sleep a little. She insists on trying to 'take care' of me. She wants to cook, clean, and wash clothes. It has been a challenge to keep her from over doing it. While I know that she can't just lay around in bed all day, it doesn't keep me from wanting to keep her there.

Charlotte has called her children every night to update them on her progress. Justin is still skeptical of me and my intentions. Charlotte has laughed off his constant questions about our housing arrangements. If he were brave enough, he would ask outright if we were having sex, but I think his mother has enough bluff on him to keep him from asking. Sara is another matter altogether. Charlotte has informed her more than once it's none of her business. We have been getting closer and closer to the final act.

Just last night we got carried away in lust. I only meant to kiss her goodnight, but my hand slipped under her t-shirt and began to gently caress her skin. My hand moved of its own accord to cup her left breast. Her nipple hardened at my touch and she arched up toward the contact. That urged me to keep going. Her breasts are large and soft. So easy to knead and squeeze. They are more than one hand can hold. Her hands are on my head. Her fingers run through my hair, encouraging me to continue my assault on her body. Lifting her shirt, my head slips under the hem to suck her right breast into my mouth. Exploding with desire, I feel her wetness on my thighs as I continue to suck and nip her nipple. My right hand is on her left breast, but I need to touch her essence. My hand leaves her left breast and she moans in protest at the loss of my hand. Her breath hitches when I slide my hand down between her thighs. I grip her mound and caress it, rubbing against her clit, briefly. My fingers slide under her damp panties and slip between her hot, wet folds. A moan escapes my throat at the feel of her slick warm channel.

"You're so wet for me." I growled. "So ready for me already."

She didn't respond with words, just bucked her hips to meet the thrust of my finger. It's still painful for her to move, but she is desperate to forget. I place my left hand over her lower abdomen and hold her still, preventing her from moving her hips. I'm not trying to be an asshole but keep her from hurting herself. My finger slides in and out of her hot core, coating it in her essence. Using her moisture as a lubricant my finger circles her clit over and over. Her release is building. The tension is easy to feel as she clamps her walls on my finger. I continue to explore her breasts with my mouth as my finger moves inside her. As she becomes wetter, I add another finger and lazily fuck her with my fingers. My thumb circles around the edge of her clit. She tries to buck her hips to create the contact she needs, but I keep her still, so she doesn't hurt herself. My hands and lips continue to build her to the boiling point. When I add a third finger to stretch her and fill her completely, she begins to quiver. I work her faster and my thumb circles her clit several times before I press into it hard. It was the final straw, she explodes on my fingers, clamping down on them until it feels as if she will cut off the blood flow, but I continue to move them in and out of her body, dragging out her release. Her head is thrown back with her eyes shut; a long loud moan escaped her throat as she was overcome in her orgasm.

She melts into the mattress as she comes back to Earth. Rolling her onto her side, I cocoon her body with mine. My arms and legs wrap around her body. We are sweaty and hot, but I need to be touching her from head to toe. The need to touch her, to consume her, is not one I am familiar with when being with a woman. But when I am with her, I can't keep my hands to myself. I had told myself to keep control, go slow, but when we are together all rational thought leaves me. My cock is itching to be inside her, but I need to slow this down. She isn't quite ready for all this. At least, I don't think she is ready. We are meant to be so I can be patient and wait for the right time.

"What about you?" She whispers into the dark when I don't try to press her for more. "I want to give you the pleasure you have given me."

"I'll be alright for now, love. You need to rest and heal, so I can take all that I want, later. I'm a patient man. I can wait until I can be inside you. I want to feel your heat and wetness around me as I pound into you. I want my dick buried in so deep that we are one when I come inside you." My voice is deep and husky with desire. It sounds obscene to me in the quite room. She nods in agreement and lets me pull her closer into my warm body heat. I thought it would be impossible to sleep, but it found us both faster than I expected.

It's going to be impossible to sleep next to her night after night, but I will because it is what she needs. Peeking into the bedroom, I see she is still sleeping. Once I am done in the bathroom, I slip into the bed and snuggle her to me. How was I ever able to sleep without her in my arms. I never liked cuddling before, but now I am more than content to do just that all night.

CHAPTER 17

CHARLOTTE

It's utterly dark. The dank smell of dirt, urine, and rot waft to my nose. The ground it cold and hard under me. I am back in the shed. No! How did this happen? Hawk came and took me away, right? Did I dream him up? Male voices are speaking Spanish. They are getting closer. Suddenly I am blinded by a bright light. A fist connects with my cheek and my head flies back. A boot kicks me hard and I can't breathe. It comes down again on my back. No! Stop! Stop! I scream. Why are you doing this to me?

"Charlotte! Wake up! You are safe. I'm here. It's me Hawk." Hawk is shaking me awake. "You're safe, love." He croons as he runs his hand down the back of my head as he tries to soothe me. My breaths are coming in short pants, sweat is beaded on my forehead. My heart racing. Shit! I was dreaming again. It's the third time tonight. I can't do this anymore. When I am fully back to myself, I seek him.

"Hawk?"

"Yes, love?"

"Will you make my fantasies come true? I need to

forget my nightmares." I whisper into the darkness of the room. He tenses and I fear his answer. He knows what I am asking. Perhaps it's too soon. I raise my head to look at his face. I am shocked at what I see. He is surprised, but I see lust and desire flood his gaze as the faint light from the bathroom lights up his face.

Without words, he lowers his lips to mine. He devours me in a slow torturous kiss. His tongue enters my mouth without asking for permission. He shifts until he is kneeling over me, straddling my waist. Holding my face in his hands, he tilts my head to the side and backward so he can deepen the kiss. I've never been kissed so fully before. He breaks the kiss and begins to move his lips down my jaw, neck, and onto my chest. He licks, nips, and kisses my skin as he makes his way lower.

Without saying a word, he reaches for the hem of my sleep shirt and proceeds to remove it. I sit up to assist him. Once it is gone. He slides his sleep pants off, raising his hips to remove them. He drops them off his side of the bed into the floor. His fingers slip under the waistband of my panties and in one swift motion they are coming off my feet. Then he is hovering over me, looking at me intensely.

"Are you sure this is what you want? Are you ready for me? Once we do this, we can't go back. I know I will sound like a dominant asshole, but you will be mine, Charlotte. All mine. No man will ever touch your body again. Are we clear?" Hawk demands of me.

"Yes, I am sure," I murmur. "As long as you are clear that you are mine. All mine. No woman will ever touch your body again. Are we clear?" I mock him even as his words have finalized the love, I feel for him. My ovaries have sat up and taken notice at his dominant words, as they say in romance novels.

"Crystal, fucking clear, love." Hawk growls as he lowers himself onto my body. Moisture floods my thighs and smell of my arousal rises in the air. His naked skin on mine feels amazing. My hands run over his back and around to his chest. I lower my hand to reach for him. His length is hard, but velvety soft. I run my fingers over the head and feel a little wetness from his precum. I long to taste him, but he grabs hand to still my movements.

"It's been a long time for me, love. And I have been hard for you for weeks. If you do that much more, this party will be over before it starts. Let me love you, then you can have your turn."

"Ok, Hawk." I feel the heat of my blush flood my face.

He kisses me tenderly, but it rapidly becomes passionate and demanding. He lowers his mouth to my right breast and sucks gently. He nips the skin along the inside and under my breast. He slowly kisses and licks his way over to my left breast and continues his ministrations. He works his way down my body, kissing, sucking, and licking. He nips the skin on my lower abdomen causing me to suck in a quick breath. He positions himself between my legs. He pushes my thighs further apart and lowers his mouth to my sex. I feel his tongue sweep between my lips and a shudder runs through me. He finds my clit. He sucks, nips, and licks me to the edge of a cliff. I am teetering on the edge. He pulls back before I can find my release. I gasp at the loss. He moves back to my mouth devouring me again.

I am on fire. I squirm and arch myself to him. I wrap my legs around him and try to get him to enter me. He chuckles.

"So damn, eager. Be patient, love. I will make you scream soon enough, but not until I am ready. I am enjoying learning your body."

"Don't tease me, Hawk. Fuck me!" I demand with almost a growl. He ignores my demands and again lowers his head to my sex and begins to assault me again. He works me to the edge again. As I feel the tension building, he slides a couple of fingers inside me as his mouth continues to torture me. I get closer to the edge. I am thrusting my hips up to meet his fingers. He adds a third finger and works me faster and harder. It only takes a few hard thrusts and I am gone. Calling his name, I shudder all over as my body clamps down on his fingers as they continue to work in and out, prolonging my release.

I slowly come back to earth. My breathing is still short and fast. He works his mouth back up my body. Once he reaches my mouth, I feel his erection head pushing against my entrance. I open my legs wider and arch my hips toward him to give him better access. He stuffs a pillow under my ass. He reaches between us, grabbing himself. He runs his head up and down my sex. Once it is soaked in my release, he slides inside me. As he hits bottom, he flexes his hips hard and bumps against my cervix. Damn that's so good. He is large and it's been a very long time, but he made sure I was ready for him. He begins to pull out and then slams back into me. I arch my hips up to meet his thrusts. We continue our dance and as the speed and fierceness increases.

I can feel the tension building in my core again. I can't believe he can make me feel all these wonderful sensations. I am wound into a frenzy. Just when I think I can't take anymore and I am going to come, he shifts his hips and hits new areas of my core as he pounds in me.

"Hawk! Oh, Hawk!" I moan. A few more thrusts are all it takes for me to burst into a million pieces. Hawk follows me over the edge a couple of thrusts later. "Charlotte!" he calls and then he arches into me, stiffening and then gives me a few more rapid thrusts. I feel him spilling into me. Finally, he is spent. He collapses onto me, being careful to not put too much pressure on my ribs. After a couple of minutes, his breathing becomes more regular. We lay this way for a long time. Later when I am almost ready to sleep, he carefully rolls us over so that I am resting on top of him. He hardness is till buried deep inside me, but it is softening. I feel the wetness of our release running out between us. Once I have enough breath to speak, I raise my head to look at him.

"That was amazing!" I say still a little breathless. His eyes are still burning with desire and I swear they are the most beautiful eyes I have ever seen. I feel like he is looking into my soul when he looks at me that way.

"Yes, it was. Give me a few minutes and we will do that again." Hawk says. He is rubbing my bare back with his calloused hands. Goosebumps break out on my skin. Is he serious? How can he want more? My arms and legs are like jelly. I am not sure I can be recovered in a few minutes. Resting my head on his chest, I let the rhythm of his heart lull me to sleep.

Sometime later I wake as I am rolled onto my back. Hawk is hard inside me again. He is slowly working himself in and out of my body. It is slow and leisurely. Nothing like the frenzy that happened earlier. He kisses and worships my body. We give each other every pleasure. Sometime later, we again explode in ecstasy. As I lay panting under him, I realize that despite all the horrors I have endured over the last few months, I am so happy to have found him.

CHAPTER 18

HAWK

LAST NIGHT WAS the most amazing experience of my life. When Charlotte woke for the third time with a nightmare, I had no idea she would be asking me to make love to her. I had intended to take things slow, but when she begged me to make her forget her nightmares there was no way I could deny her request.

Her hot body had been much more than my fantasies or dreams had imagined. She was wet for me instantly. She eagerly tried to take me inside her. It was important to me that she have what she needed. Making her come before I entered her body was a must. She had not kept it a secret that she had not had sex since before her husband had died. Five years is a long time and I didn't want to hurt her. I shouldn't have worried. She took everything I gave her and gave as good as she got.

I am so in over my head with this woman. Her body is an addiction. Now that we have crossed that line, I'm not sure I can ever get enough. She had only been asleep for an hour when I could wait no longer to take her again. She didn't seem to mind as I rolled her onto her back to take her again. Her hips met mine thrust for thrust. She is a wildcat in bed just as I had suspected. I am eager to learn more about her and her body.

It crosses my mind that we didn't use a condom, but we are both clean so no need to worry about that. Perhaps I should be worried about impregnating her, but if she were carrying my child, I would be the happiest man alive. I never thought I would want more children after all that happened with Julie. However, the thought of Charlotte round with my child makes me feel complete and satisfied.

Charlotte is still sleeping so I slip out of bed and head into the kitchen to fix her coffee and some breakfast. She likes to cook with me, but this morning I want to spoil her. Breakfast in bed is just what she needs. It's the least I can do for her after she gave herself to me so freely. I keep thinking I should be worried we are moving too fast, but her words from a few nights ago flash in my mind.

"Hawk we are not kids; we are adults. I think we have seen and done enough that we can know what we want. Because we are older, we realize that we don't have unlimited time. Life is short and it can be gone in the blink of an eye. After the summer I have had, I will no longer spend time worrying if I should do something or what others think about what I am doing. If it's something I want, I am going to go for it. If I wait, it could be gone forever."

Charlotte is right. We don't have unlimited time together. If Hugo Lopez has anything to say about it, she could be gone from me tomorrow. Not that I or my team would let him get away with it, but there is no promise of tomorrow. We need to make the most of our time together. It crosses my mind she might come to her senses and want to go home to her children, friends, and career. It would be the hardest thing to do, to let her go, but I would never keep her against her will. I'm not sure how I would make it if she left me.

Determined to make her never want to leave me, I take her breakfast into our bedroom. She is the most beautiful woman I have laid eyes on. She is laying on her side with her back to me. The covers have slid down her body to about mid waist. As I round the bed, I take in the glorious site in front of me. Her brown curly hair is spread out over the pillows and her hands are tucked between her face and the pillow. Her breasts are playing peek-a-boo between her arms as her chest rises and falls with her breathing. Her face is so relaxed. Angelic. That is what comes to mind as I gaze down on her.

She wakes easily as I sit on the side of the bed after placing our breakfast tray on the bedside table. Her eyes fly open and when she recognizes me, her face transforms from confusion to pure bliss. Is that love I see in her eyes? Her whole face lights up with her smile that brightens her greenish-brown eyes causing the golden flecks to sparkle in the morning light. My heart lurches as I realize I want this for the rest of my life. I want ***her*** in my bed, in my life. I love her. It has happened so fast, but I have no doubts about what I am feeling for her.

"Good morning, love." I can hardly speak with the lump in my throat at my sudden realization. The smile on my face is most likely going to scare her away but I couldn't stop smiling if my life depended on it. She returns my smile, but then as if she remembers what we did last night her face flushes the cutest shade of red.

"Um...good morning." She has looked away from me and seeing her naked body. She jerks the cover over her chest and tries to sit up. She face is now a dark red and her chest is rising up and down in her discomfort.

"Don't ever be embarrassed about making love with me." I gently chastise her. Her eyes met mine then. It's like she is looking into my soul to see if I mean what I am saying. She must have seen what she was looking for as she nods in agreement and scoots over so I can sit beside her on the bed. We eat in a comfortable silence. When we have finished, I place the tray on the bedside table. I reach for her hand and she immediately places her small hand in mine.

"Come on, love. We need a shower." I pull her out from under the covers and into the bathroom. Goosebumps have erupted on her skin. I'm not sure if it's desire or the loss of heat from the cover. Perhaps a combination of both. She is so reactive to my touch and it makes me even more possessive. Her body is mine, all mine. After all she agreed last night before I took her.

The shower is warm. I take the liberty of washing her hair and body just as I did in the Columbian safe house. This time I allow her to return the favor. Her hands on my body cause a natural reaction. It is surprising that at my age I am able to have such an acute response again so soon. But there is no way I could control it. When her petite hands move up my legs soaping them as she goes, my dick stands at attention wanting her hands on it.

As if she can read my mind, they are there caressing it from base to tip. The soap on her hands aid her movements. She momentarily steps to the side to allow the shower to rinse the soap away. Then she is on her knees and has sucked my dick into her mouth before I can register what she had in mind. Her mouth is warm on my skin. She slides me slowly in and out a couple of times letting her lips rub from tip to almost the base. I feel the head of dick bump the back of her throat with each pass. On the third pass, she begins to suck on me as she takes me in. I can't choke back the groan that escapes my lips.

Her eyes dart to mine and she smiles around my dick as she continues to suck on it as she takes it further in her mouth. She continues to go down on me slow and steady. Pre-cum is leaking into her mouth, but she continues her attention. The need to be inside her hot channel when I come is overwhelming. Looking down I realize my hands are in her hair encouraging her to keep going. I pull her head back until she releases me. She raises her eyes in surprise.

"I want to be inside you when I cum, love." Reaching behind her, I turn off the water and grab a towel. I quickly dry us off and taking her hand I drag her into the bedroom. My lips have found hers and I back her into the bed. She falls back with a shriek of surprise. As I crawl onto the bed, she scoots back toward the head and center of the bed. She opens herself to me with arms and legs spread wide so I can lay down on top of her. It is Heaven to be in her warm arms.

"Roll over, love. I want to take you from behind." A worried look crosses over her face and it gives me pause. "What's wrong? Did I hurt you?" I am not sure what has happened, but she has stiffened her movements and looks worried and unsure.

"Um…nothing's wrong." She starts to turn away from me when I stop her. Her eyes meet mine with uncertainty. Tears are beginning to well in her eyes. Something is definitely wrong.

"Charlotte, talk to me. What did I say or do wrong?"

"It's nothing…I…I've just never… Until you, my husband was my only lover. We weren't adventurous in bed. He didn't like going down on me even though he liked it when I did it for him. We mostly only did missionary and cowgirl. I never felt comfortable doggy style." Her voice quavers. "It seems so impersonal. That's what Tweedledee was going to do to me. Do you not want to look at me?" Tears are now falling down her face. She thinks I don't want to look at her. She couldn't be any more wrong. I just need to show her.

"Charlotte, love. I love looking at you. You face, your body." Taking her face in my hands I place a gentle kiss on her lips. "I promise anything we do will be anything, but impersonal. It's just a different position." She is looking at me so trustingly. "Don't let him in our bed, love. Let me show you how good this can be." Rolling her onto her stomach, she comes up on her hands and knees. Wanting to make sure she is ready for me; I kneel behind her and take in the scent of her arousal. She looks back at me over her shoulder her eyes wide. "Are you smelling me?" she asks disbelievingly.

"Yes, I am, and you smell amazing. Just your scent almost undid me. That smell makes me remember how hot, tight, and wet you are." Done talking, I lean into her hot sex and lick from one end to the other. She shivers under my tongue and I smile. She's going to like this. Feasting on her like this is amazing. She is dripping wet and the more I touch her the more she moves. She is basically fucking herself on my face and her juices are all over my beard and mustache. When she is quaking about to fall over the edge, I raise up and inch my hips closer to her. My hardened length slips inside her hot depths. We moan at the same time as I bottom out inside her.

Leaning back on my heels, I take her with me. Her legs are spread wide and she comes up on her knees only. Her hands grip my arms as I steady her by I wrapping my arms around her chest cupping her breasts. Her head falls back onto my right shoulder. Lowering my right hand to her clit, I begin to rub it slowly. She jerks at my touch.

"That's it, love. Ride me," My hands move to her hips to raise and lower her on my dick.

"Lean forward so we can move, baby." She falls back onto her hands and I follow her down. Leaning over her back I continue to manipulate her clit and left nipple with my hands while my hips pump in and out of her. She is meeting my actions by pushing her hips toward me with every thrust. The more we move the harder the thrust. The slapping of flesh on flesh and our moans are the only sounds in the room. She comes hard after a few moments and I am grateful. I'm not 18 anymore and the third time in about 12 hours, I'm not lasting long. My hands move to her hips as I pound into her. I follow her over the edges as she strangles my dick with her hot pussy walls. We collapse on the bed in exhaustion. Chuckling it occurs to me we need to shower again as we are covered in sweat and sex again. We don't have any appointments today, so sleep comes again in moments.

CHAPTER 19

CHARLOTTE

THE RINGING of Hawk's phone wakes me from sleep. It is late morning if the light coming in the window is any indication. His breath hits the back of my neck as he huffs out a sigh. He untangles himself from me as he twists around to get his phone off the nightstand on his side of the bed. I whine and try to snuggle back into him. My body is still like Jell-O from the multiple orgasms he has given me over night and early this morning. He picks up the phone looking at the screen and frowns. As he answers the phone, he settles back on the bed and snakes his left arm around me, pulling me to him. I sigh contentedly and snuggle into his side.

"Hawk here. What's up, Captain?" Hawk asks as he answers the phone. He looks down at me, smiles, then places a kiss on my temple. I draw little circles in his chest hair while he listens to the Captain. I can't hear what is being said, but I feel Hawk tense. Something is upsetting him. I raise my head to look at him and see if I can tell from his expression what is wrong.

"What? How the hell did they find out she is here?" Hawk demands. "Have we got a leak? Or is the pentagon trying to get some positive publicity. Some damn Senator up for re-election?" Hawk seems pissed. Who could know that I am here? Only my kids know where I am recovering.

"Do you think that is wise?" Hawk asks. There is a pause. "I understand. I know it would make the press even more curious. Ok, we are just getting up. She's still having trouble sleeping. Give me an hour." Hawk clicks the phone off.

"What's wrong? Who knows I'm here?" I ask running my hand over his chest trying to soothe him. I don't want him to be upset, especially over me. Hawk turns to me. He places his hand on my face.

"It seems some of your friends are here and they are demanding to see you. Captain tried to convince them that you aren't here, but they insist they have it on good authority that you are here. So, we are going to get ready, eat again, and go see who these people are."

"Ok" I move to leave the bed. Hawk reaches for me. He pulls me to him and kisses me passionately. He sighs deeply. He looks at me so intensely. I try to figure out what he's thinking. "Come on love. Let's get this over with."

We shower and dress quickly. Then we eat a quick snack. My mind is racing trying to figure out who could be here to see me. How did anyone find out? My kids would not tell anyone. They know how important it is to keep my story out of the news, at least until the SEALs can complete their mission. All the time and effort they have put in would be wasted, not to mention it could endanger the soldier's lives.

Once we are ready to go, Hawk calls Ace who shows up in a few minutes in a SUV to take us to the command center on base. When we get there, Deadeye, Straw, Tank, Mercury, and Wallace meet us at the door. They surround me as we enter the complex and move toward the conference room. We stop outside the door. Hawk and Deadeye insist on going in first to assess the situation. They return a few minutes later with Captain Olson.

"Charlotte, there are some people here that claim they know you. A Dr. George Jones, a Lisa Winters, and a JoAnn Walters." Captain Olson explains. "Do you know these people?"

"Yes, they are my co-workers and were my traveling companions to Guatemala." I am in shock that they are actually here. How did they find out that I was here? What will they think? Are they upset with me about wondering off and getting taken? Why am I even worrying about what they think? I am the one that suffered so much, but it's in my nature to worry about everyone, but me.

"You don't have to see them, but I think it would be best to assure them that you are ok." Captain Olson tells me. "I think that Dr Jones will have *48 hours* on us if we don't let them see that you are safe and are being cared for."

"It's fine Captain Olson. I will talk to them," I reply. Hawk takes my hand then and leads me into the conference room. Dr Jones, Lisa, and JoAnn are sitting on the far side of the table. Virus, Hack, and Worm are standing against the far wall. As we enter the room, Dr Jones jumps to his feet and rounds the table. Heading for me, Hawk immediately pushes me behind him as Ace and Deadeye move to restrain Dr Jones.

“What the hell is going on?” Dr Jones demands. “Why are you keeping her away from us?”

“Calm down, Dr Jones. We aren’t trying to keep her away from anyone,” Captain Olson says as he enters the room behind us. “Charlotte has been through quiet an ordeal. She is still healing. The guys are just trying to keep you from causing her pain, by your over zealousness.”

Dr Jones stops his struggling. He peers around Ace’s shoulder. “Charlotte? Are you alright?”

“Yes, I’m fine Dr. Jones.” I say as I start around Hawk, but he keeps me behind him. “I’m still healing. I had some broken ribs. It’s still difficult to get around. The guys were afraid you would try to hug me or something and it would hurt me. They are just protecting me.”

“How about we sit down? We can let you all visit a few minutes.” Captain Olson says in a soothing, but commanding tone.

Lisa is coming toward me slowly. I reach out for her and she grips my hand. Tears fill my eyes as she begins to cry. I place my arms around her. She gently hugs me back.

“I was so worried. I thought we would never see you again,” Lisa whispers to me.

“I know.” It’s all I can manage to say. My throat is tight with emotion. All the time I was in captivity, I had wondered if I would ever see them again. Hawk places his hands on my shoulders. I look over my shoulder to look at him. He motions me to sit at the table. We move to the table and Hawk helps me to sit. He takes the chair next to mine and places his hand on my knee under the table. Dr. Jones is eyeing us with concern.

“Charlotte, tell me what is going on here. Why didn’t

you come home once you were back?" Dr Jones asks irritation easy to hear in his tone.

"Charlotte was severely injured. She spent several days in the hospital." Hawk answers for me. He is tense. His hand is tightening on my knee as he speaks. "She needs to recover before she can travel. Her doctors have recommended she remain close so they can follow up with her. She needs to see them frequently."

"I had a collapsed lung, multiple contusions, lacerations, rib fractures, and a head injury. The doctors have advised that I remain here close to them for follow up," I try to explain to placate Dr Jones.

"That is of no consequence. I can arrange a medical transport for her to return home. She needs to be with her family and friends. I will arrange for whatever specialists you need, Charlotte." Dr Jones practically growls at Hawk. As if he didn't even hear what I said.

"She is not going anywhere!" Hawk almost shouts. He is definitely pissed. I reach over and place my hand on his face.

"It's ok Hawk, I am not going anywhere," I say to reassure him.

"Charlotte, what are you saying? Of course, you are coming home as soon as I can arrange it," Dr Jones says with conviction. I can feel the tension building in the room. The Marines are on edge. Dr Jones looks like he is going to burst a blood vessel. Lisa and JoAnn are looking on in confusion. They look from Dr Jones to me and Hawk.

"Dr Jones, I appreciate your concern, but I don't think going home is the right thing to do at the moment. I need time to process everything that has happened to me. I need time to heal," I declare. "My psychiatrist is here. I am not ready to deal with the press. They will be hounding me if they know where I am. There are some very bad men that are still looking for me. I just can't deal with that right now. Captain Olson and Hawk are making sure I am safe and protected."

"A psychiatrist? What the hell happened down there? Where did you go? We got up and you were just gone. We looked everywhere and couldn't find any trace of you," Dr Jones demands. "Why did you wander off and get yourself kidnapped?"

"Are you fucking serious? You are blaming her for being kidnapped and tortured for months?" Hawk yells. "Some friends you are."

"What were we supposed to think? You disappear in the middle of the night. Nothing was out of place. We all know how you have trouble sleeping. What did you do, decide to go for a walk and get lost? You have always thrived on attention," JoAnn speaks up. She had been unusually quite while the drama was unfolding.

"What the Hell JoAnn?" Lisa yells at her. "You can't be serious. Charlotte wouldn't purposefully put herself in harms way and you damn well know it."

"Oh, come on Lisa. Charlotte is always doing something to get attention." JoAnn sneers.

Hawk jumps to his feet, taking my hand and urging me to my feet. "We are done here. You have seen she's alive, so we are leaving. You will go back to Hicksville, USA and live your lives. You will not tell anyone where Charlotte is or there will be serious consequences. Are we clear?" Hawk has me on my feet now and he's moving us toward the door. Ace, and the others move in behind us forming a protective barrier.

"Is this for real?" Dr Jones shouts. "I have connections. I will go to the damn White House if I have to. You can't keep her hostage."

"I am not hostage," I assert. "I understand you are confused about everything that has happened. Hell, I lived it and I am still struggling with it. I need to stay here. I'm not going to explain to you why, but I do. I will be coming back home at some point, but for right now. I am where I am supposed to be." The stress from this confrontation and in my weakened condition it all just becomes too much. I feel myself falter, but before I can hit the floor, Hawk has once again swept me up off my feet.

"Captain, I need to get her home. She's over done it. She needs to rest," Hawk looks at me with concern. He is already heading for the door.

"Alright, Hawk. Take care of her. I will talk to you later," Captain Olson dismisses us. Straw opens the door of the conference room and Hawk carries me out to the waiting SUV. I feel bad that they are so upset, but I just can't go back right now. I am afraid. I'm afraid of Lopez's men finding me and taking me back to Hell. I'm scared that I will lose control again without Hawk to bring me back to reality. I cling to Hawk like the lifeline he is as he settles me on to his lap in the back seat. I lay my head on his shoulder and close my eyes. While we wait for the others to pile into the SUV.

"I'm so sorry, love." Hawk whispers in my ear. "I should never have allowed this to happen. I knew you weren't up to a confrontation. We should have told those fuckers to fuck off." Hawk growls in frustration. I raise my head up and place a gentle kiss on his cheek. He looks down at me with such tenderness in his eyes. I smile at him. I want to assure him that I am going to be fine. Hawk settles me into the seat and buckles my seatbelt.

Ace is behind the wheel with Deadeye riding shotgun. Tank has climbed in beside me. The others follow us in another vehicle. Once we arrive back at the house, Hawk carries me back inside and puts me to bed. The others set up watch in case my friends try to find me. I am out before my head hits the pillow.

CHAPTER 20

CHARLOTTE

Wakefulness comes to me. My bindings are gone and I'm no longer on the ground. I'm in a bed, where am I? Suddenly, a blinding light pierces my eyes. It's happening again. They are coming to hurt me again. I have to get away. Scrambling to get off the bed, I hit the floor hard on my right side. Pain shoots through my chest. God it hurts so bad to breathe. They are coming! The footsteps getting closer. I crawl under the bed to hide. A whimper escapes my lips, hush, be quiet, or they will find me. I try to make myself as small as possible. Hands are grabbing on to me, pulling me back. I kick, scream, and fight like hell to get away. I can't let them do this anymore.

"Charlotte! Please stop fighting. It's me. Hawk. Come back to me, love." I hear the words, but it can't be true. Is my dream really here? He can't be here. I'm hallucinating again. Why can't this be over?

"No! Stop! Please don't hurt me anymore," I sob as tears streak my face. I have tried not to let them see me cry. It only gives them pleasure to know they are hurting me, but I can't stop the flow.

"You're safe. Charlotte. I'm here. I won't let anyone hurt you." His deep soothing voice is in my ear and I want to believe him. It needs to be real. Looking around at the arms holding me, I trail them up to his face. It's him. He's here? Where are we? How did he find me? Touching his face frowning, he feels real.

"You're here? How is that possible?" I whisper.

"Yes, I'm here, love. You are safe. I got you out of the jungle. Remember? We are in California, on base." Hawk tells me patiently. He runs his hands over my back. Looking around, letting my eyes adjust to the light coming from the door. Behind me I see the bed where Hawk made love to me. Over Hawk's shoulder, I see the bathroom where we showered just hours ago. It's real? We are safe, in the house on base. Oh, God! I'm losing my mind. It was so real that I was still in that awful shed. Trembling I fall into his arms. Now he knows just how messed up I am.

"Charlotte? Are you hurt? That was a hard fall you took from the bed." Hawk is running his hands over me checking for injuries. I want to just fall apart, but I know that if I allow myself to break, I will not be able to come back. I cling to him. He is my lifeline to reality.

"No, I'm not hurt." I reply. He helps me up and I don't protest when he puts me back into bed. I close my eyes and feign sleep. It's just too embarrassing to deal with right now. I just need some time to get my mind cleared. He gets up from the edge of the bed. Instinctively I reach out and grab his hand. He can't leave me. If I go back there again and he isn't here to bring me back, I'll be stuck there forever. "Don't leave me, please?" I plead. It makes me sound weak and needy. Perhaps, I am. My hope is that he wants to be here for me, that he doesn't see me as a burden. I hate that I am forced to admit weakness, but I know that I need him above all else.

"I won't, love. I'm going to get your supper. I'll be right back." Hawk assures me in a soothing voice one would use to deal with a frightened child. Nodding I watch as he heads out the door. A few short minutes later he returns with a tray laden down with sandwiches, fresh veggies, fresh fruits, and assorted cheeses. He brings the tray over to sit it beside me. He begins to feed me as he did while in the safe house in Columbia. Where would I be if he hadn't found me?

After eating, Hawk takes the tray back down the hall. When he returns, he has company. Deadeye, Ace, Wallace, Virus, Hack, Worm, Tank, Mercury, and Straw follow him into the room. They look at me suspiciously, but also with concern. They must think I am broken and I'm sure they are worried about Hawk being mixed up with a crazy person. The men have brought chairs in and they are sitting in a semi-circle around the bed, while some stand along the wall.

"Hey, sweetheart. How are you feeling?" Deadeye asks. He looks at me intensely, trying to determine if I am in reality or if I'm back in the Columbian jungle.

"I'm not sure." I answer honestly. "I think I might be broken."

"I don't think your broken, darling. Maybe a little bruised." Worm says.

"What he means to say is that you just need a little help to get past all this." Ace says with a smile. "We want to help you. But you have to be honest with us. Hawk is too close to you to be objective. I need you to tell me what has been happening in your head since we got back. You are going to see the doctor and you are going to tell them honestly what is happening with you."

"That's enough Ace. What the hell is wrong with you? She has been through enough already." Hawk rants as he comes to sit with me. He runs his hand through his hair in frustration.

"Hawk, he's right. I haven't been completely honest." I say as I take a deep shuttering breath. "I feel like I am back there sometimes. I see, feel, and even smell the dirt floor. I hear them coming for me. I can feel their fists, their boots. I know what they are going to do. I am overtaken with fear. I haven't been able to get myself back to reality. Only you have been able to bring me back."

"I know you were out of it before when you woke. Has it happened before?" Hawk asks me.

"Yes, the night at the hospital when I told you I fell out of bed. I heard some men speaking Spanish in the hallway, then a bright light hit me. It was just like when I was captive. It was always so dark, but the bright light would blind me and then the pain would come. It happened over and over every day was the same. What if next time I can't come back? I can't live in that Hell. I would rather die."

"That is not going to happen." Straw declares firmly. "We are going to help you. The first step was admitting that you are having more than nightmares. Now we just have to help keep you grounded and prevent triggering flashbacks. Dr. Hancock can help you."

"From what you have told us, a bright light seems to bring about the flashbacks. It happened at the hospital and again this afternoon. So, we keep a night light on in here. You need to make sure you stay with one of us at all times." Wallace says.

"I know you won't like this idea, but for your safety it needs to happen." Deadeye says giving me a stern look. "You need to let us put some trackers on you, in your clothes and personal belongings. It might sound creepy, but if something happens when we aren't around then we can still find you."

"You want to chip me, like a dog?" I ask incredulously. "I can't believe you are serious!"

"It's not like that, love." Hawk says quietly. "They wouldn't be placed under your skin like an animal but would be placed in your clothing, jewelry, maybe your purse. We would be able to track you through your with it. Wolf told me how they used them to find Benny and his woman when they were abducted by a madman. It saved their lives." I ponder on this for a moment.

"I need a little time to think about this, Ok? I'm not saying I won't agree to it. I just need some time to think it through." I tell the group of men. Seeing the concern and fear in their eyes, I know that I should trust them to do what is best for me. After all, they got me out of the Columbian jungle when no one even knew where I was. Still, it's unnerving to think that my every move could be tracked.

As I am pondering the implications of wearing trackers, Tank speaks up. "Virus, have you heard anymore chatter on the net from the Lopez brothers?"

"Not anything new. The chatter is about the same. Everyone discussing where they think she could be hiding. Most think she has gone back to Kentucky, but there were posts today saying she couldn't be there, or the press would be getting interviews." Virus replies.

"Surprisingly these criminals are actually kind of smart." Hack comments. "I'm surprised they could deduce something like that." While I am thankful for the change in conversation, this is still not one I want to have. The guys continue to discuss the events of the day from my visitors to my freak out spell. By the time they have finished, I am feeling a little better. None of them have made me feel like I am crazy or a burden. After the deep conversation is over, the guys get up, gather their chairs, and head for the door. Hawk gets up to follow them out the door.

"I'll be right back, love." Hawk assures me as he follows them out into the main part of the house. I decide to head into the bathroom and get ready for the battle ahead that night has become for me. After brushing my teeth and washing my face I put on a tank top and shorts set. By the time I emerge from the bathroom, Hawk is sitting on the bed studying his hands. He looks up as I enter the room.

"Hey, love. You ready for bed?" Hawk asks quietly. I nod. He is afraid I am upset about the trackers. I should make him squirm a little after all that is a little creepy, but I just can't. It is because he wants to keep me safe that he even mentioned it.

"Yeah, I'm ready." I climb into my side of the bed. Hawk gets up and heads into the bathroom. He returns a little while later. I am already beginning to feel sleepy, but I want to assure him that I am not upset about the trackers, but the fact that I would even need one. Hawk leaves the bathroom light on and walks around the bed to climb in on his side of the bed. He lays on his back and remains quiet. After several minutes, I reach over and take his hand in mine. Turning my head to the right so I can look at him.

"Hawk, I will wear the trackers." I whisper into the quiet of the night. "I'm not upset that you asked me to wear them, but I am upset that I ***need*** to wear them. I know that you are only trying to keep me safe. I appreciate that and I am thankful. I know it's in my best interest. If I go off the rails or if Lopez gets his hands on me, you will be able to find me and reel me back to reality."

Hawk just squeezes my hand. He turns to me and motions for me to turn over, so my back is to his front. It's his and if I'm honest my favorite sleeping position. We lay there for a long time, before sleep comes. Both of us wondering what the night will bring.

CHAPTER 21

HAWK

CHARLOTTE'S FLASHBACK scared the shit out of me. What happens next time? What if I can't bring her back to me? Can I handle having to put her in the hospital while we get her mind to a better place? I have never had to deal with anything like this. I feel so inadequate. I won't give up on her no matter how hard this gets. I'm going to talk with Dr Hancock tomorrow at her therapy appointment. There has to be more we can do to help her.

She is consuming my every thought. I can't stand the thoughts of being without this woman at my side. I am praying with all that I have, she doesn't wake up and decide she wants to go back home to her children, job, and friends. I need her like I need air. She seems to feel the same. It's in her eyes when she looks at me. She stares at me through her lashes. She tries to not let me see her staring, but I see the desire, wonder, and dare I hope love in her eyes. It's too soon to be thinking she could be in love with me, but I know how I feel about her. There is love at first sight, right?

Holding her while she sleeps with her body curled

into mine is what I love. We are touching from neck to toes. Her back is pressed into the muscles of my chest. Her body rises and falls with her steady breathing. My arm is laced over her waist and my hand is cupping her breast. I shouldn't grope her while she sleeps but it's like instinct for my hand to wander its way up her body and rest against the perfect globes. Her glorious ass is pressed hard against my groin. If I think about this too much, I'm going to be hard again.

She is going to be the death of me. My body craves hers. I need to touch, feel, and taste her essence. I am going to have terminal blue balls if this keeps up. I want to take her, but she is sleeping so peacefully. I don't have the heart to wake her even to relive my discomfort. The nightmares will start again soon; I can wait, until she asks me to take her away again. She said I kept her sane during her torture, because she fantasied about me. She had dreamed of me making love to her, rescuing her, and saving her from the nightmare. So, when they come again, I will bring her dreams to life. I will love and worship her body so thoroughly the nightmares will leave, never to return.

The next morning after breakfast, the familiar sound of a Facetime call sounds from my phone. I ask Charlotte to sit with me while I take this call from home. It's time she gets to meet my parents and my son. Swiping my phones screen to accept the call, I brace for the onslaught of my family.

"Hello!" I say as I look at the screen. My Dad's smiling face greets me.

"Good morning, son. How are things going out there?" Dad inquires. "We hadn't heard from you in a few days, just thought I would check in."

"Good morning, Dad," I smile at him through the

phone. "Things are pretty good. I want you to meet someone. Say hi to Charlotte." I turn the phone so that the camera is pointed at Charlotte.

"Hello, Charlotte. It's nice to finally meet you. Jordan has told me lots of good things about you." Dad is beaming through the phone. He can be quite the charmer when he wants to be.

"Hi, Mr. Jackson," Charlotte's blush is so cute. It's endearing that a grown woman can blush at such a simple compliment. "It's nice to meet you, too. Hawk has told me all about you, your wife, and Brian."

"Don't believe everything he tells you," Dad chuckles. "We aren't all bad."

"Dad, you are going to alarm the poor woman," I gently chastise my Dad. "I haven't told her the bad stuff yet. I didn't want to scare her off." I chuckle before asking about Brian. "Where's my boy this morning?"

"He had football practice this morning, so your mother took him and left me to my own devices," Dad laughs at his joke. "I have managed to behave myself so far. At least the house is still standing."

"Ha, Ha," I reply sarcastically. "You are the only one out of the whole family I would trust to be left at home alone and the house remain standing." Dad's eyes dance with amusement.

"You are just saying that because you have company," Dad smiles back at me. I laugh at Dad's attempt to joke with me.

"Have Brian give me a call later when he gets home. It's been a couple of days since I have Facetimed him. This texting just isn't the same as seeing him." Dad nods in agreement.

"I know what you mean. That boy has dragged your mother and I into the 21st Century kicking and screaming." Dad laughs out loud. "Some days I think we are too old to learn this shit…excuse me Charlotte, stuff, but at least we aren't lost when he's talking about Instagram and Twitter." Charlotte giggles at Dad's slip. He rarely says a curse word in front of a woman.

"I'm sorry, Dad. You know I'm grateful to you and Mom for everything." It guts me sometimes to think about how much they have sacrificed for us. I wouldn't want Brian with anyone else, but I still feel guilty that they have given up so much of their retirement to help me raise him. Charlotte gets up and motions she is going to sit outside in the backyard while I talk with my father. I nod in understanding as she leaves the room.

"Jordan," Dad's voice is stern. "Don't start that again. We wouldn't change a thing. You know that."

"Yeah, Dad. I know and I really appreciate it, more than you will ever know," the need to change the subject prompts my next question. "It'll be deer season soon. Are you getting geared up for that?"

"Yeah, Jason, Joseph, Marcus, Brian, and I are planning to hit it opening weekend of gun season. Do you think you'll be back by then?" Dad asks. His face is frowned in concern. I know they worry about me when I'm away from home. "We have a tree stand with your name on it."

"No promises, but I hope so." Dad knows how it is when you serve. After all he was in for 30 years, before he retired to pursue other interests. He worked as a deputy sheriff for several years before entering full retirement. Mom has always been a stay at home housewife, but no one has worked harder than she has. She's active in church, volunteers at the local hospital and nursing home, and still had time for her family, never missing a game or PTA meeting.

"Say, Dad. I was hoping to talk to you about something." I pause as I try to gather my thoughts.

"Of course, Jordan. You know you can talk to me about anything." Dad looks concerned. It's not often that I seek his advice at my age, but I need to tell someone about the budding relationship between Charlotte and me.

"Dad…I am falling for Charlotte." I decide the best way is to just lay it out there.

"I'm happy for you son." Dad's face softens. "It's about time you found a good woman. Your mother and I were worried that after Julie you wouldn't ever give love another chance. For what it's worth, from what you have told me and meeting her, Charlotte seems like a good person. Don't let the fear of the past get in the way of your future."

"Thanks Dad. I won't. For the first time in years, I want a future, to build a family for Brian, maybe give him some siblings. She's it for me. Destiny laid her in my lap and I'm not going to mess this up."

"Good. Call your mother later. She will have a fit she missed getting to talk to you."

"I will, Dad. Take care and I'll talk to you soon," I end the call and head outside to find my woman. Time to move this relationship forward.

CHAPTER 22

CHARLOTTE

Two months have passed in the blink of an eye. I had daily therapy sessions with Dr Hancock at first then three times a week for a few weeks, now only weekly. She has really helped me to come to terms with the torture I endured. It's getting better every day. The nightmares are not as frequent. I only wake a couple of times a week now. I haven't had any serious flashbacks in over a week. Tex sent the trackers. I always have a least two on me. I have gotten to know Caroline and the other women better. We have had lunch a several of times and spent a whole day shopping together. They have all been so nice to me and made me feel welcome.

I have been to several "debriefing" meetings to tell what I know about Hugo Lopez. Apparently, he was the man I overheard talking about kidnapping border officers' family members. The government has intervened and so far, no one has been kidnapped. Captain Olson and Commander Hurt are convinced that I am still in danger. They heard chatter that Lopez is looking for an American woman that was taken from his brother by

American soldiers. He has a $100,000 bounty out for me. He knows that I helped to derail his plans at the border, and he wants revenge.

Hawk has refused to let me out of his sight after getting that little piece of intel. Captain Olson assures us that we are safe while on base but doesn't recommend my going home to visit, yet. He offers to bring the kids out again, but I don't want them missing any more time from work. I talk and Facetime them daily. I am getting restless though. I need to get back to work. I miss taking care of my patients. I don't really need the money. My house is paid for and I have several CDs that deposit the interest into my checking every month. My husband's life insurance made sure I would be taken care of at his death.

I am totally in love with Hawk, though I haven't told him. I know that only knowing him for a few months that it is crazy to be in love, but I know in my heart he is my soulmate. I love him more than I ever knew I could love someone. We have been inseparable since I was discharged from the hospital. He is so affectionate. He is constantly holding my hand, touching my hair, or placing a gentle hand at the small of my back as he leads me wherever we may be going. He insists on opening the car door for me, buckling my seatbelt, and always helps me in and out of any vehicle we ride in. As my ribs have mostly healed, our love life has blossomed. I didn't know I could enjoy sex so much. I crave it. I go to sleep sated each night, but by morning I am craving him again. I can't get enough.

My kids are getting impatient for me to come back home. I have explained to them that until things are resolved with the gun runners and I no longer need to see Dr Hancock so frequently I need to stay here. It's time to figure out what I am going to do. I don't want to leave Hawk, but can I really move to California? I'm conflicted. I know that if I explain how I feel about him to my kids they will understand, but I need to know that Hawk is really serious about us.

While in the kitchen cooking supper, I am looking out into the backyard thinking about where our relationship is going when I feel strong arms wrap around my waist. Smiling I lean back into his embrace. He rocks me gently.

"What are you thinking so hard about love?" Hawk whispers in my ear. "You seem so serious."

"Us." I say quietly. "What do you see in our future?" I am afraid of what he will say, but its past time to have this conversation. I need to know what he is thinking, so I can decide what I need to do.

Hawk freezes and tenses briefly before turning me around in his embrace. He has his arms draped loosely around my waist. My arms are resting on his. He has his lower body pressed into mine. I am pinned between him and the kitchen counter. He has the most intense look in his eyes that I have ever seen. His eyes bore into mine. It's like he can see into my soul. I search his eyes, trying to read his mind. I need to know what is going on in his brain.

"I see us together. I see us making a life together, a family. I have no intention of letting you get away from me, Charlotte." Hawk says with conviction. "I meant what I said in Columbia. I feel a connection to you. I want to be with you for the rest of my life. I love you. What do you see, love?"

"Oh Hawk. You love me?"

"Yeah, love. I love you. I think I have been in love since I kissed your hand in the airport café." Hawk's voice is low and husky. It sends butterflies to my sex and wetness pools. Damn, I am horny all the time around this man.

"I love you, too. That's what I want too. I just needed to know you felt the same. I know we have talked about it some at first, but you didn't really know me. I just needed reassurance you still felt the same way." I sigh as I realize that he does care for me and is not planning on dumping me once I am sane again.

"I want you to understand. I am never going to let you go. Don't ever doubt me again." Hawk says sternly. "I asked you if you were sure about us, before I made love to you the first time. I told you once we crossed that line, you were mine."

"I know. I just let my insecurities get the better of me sometimes. I'm sorry I doubted you. You haven't done anything to make me question you."

"I want to build a life with you. I don't know how you feel about having more children, but if you are open to it. I am. I know that we are getting a bit old to be having kids, but I love kids and you having mine would be amazing." Hawk says earnestly.

"Hawk? Really? You want us to have a baby? I might be getting too old for that, but if it happened, I would be overjoyed." I reply with tears forming in my eyes. The tears seem to come to easily in the last week. I had thought I was getting better, but the water works have started again.

"Well now that is settled. Let's eat. I'm starving. Wolf and Caroline want us to come to Aces bar for drinks later. All the guys, SEALs, and their women will be there."

"That sounds like fun." I smile at him. He lowers his head and steals a quick kiss. I pull him back to my mouth before he can pull away. I kiss him deeply, relishing in his taste. He is such a good kisser. His tongue enters my mouth and dances with mine for several long minutes. Finally, he pulls back, laughing.

"We are going to be late meeting the guys if you keep that up."

"Ok, I'll behave. We will take this up later, though." I smile turning back to finish supper.

A couple of hours later, we arrive at *Aces Bar and Grill*. Hawk is dressed in kakis and a dark green polo shirt. His muscles bulge and flex as he moves. He is looking so damn good. Several women turn to look at him as we cross the dance floor. I feel the green monster of jealously rearing its ugly head, but I relax when he puts his arm around my waist. He pulls me close to his side and places a kiss on my temple.

At Hawk's insistence, I have on a little black dress. He actually picked it out the last time we went shopping. It is a halter dress with a built-in bra. It has a little too much v in the front. I feel like my boobs are going to fall out at any moment. The back scoops low showing way more skin than I am comfortable with, but Hawk assured me that I look gorgeous. Thankfully, the hem comes to my knees. I have on matching black pumps. Before we left, Hawk gave me a beautiful necklace with a single tear drop diamond, that is resting at the top of my cleavage. My hair has cooperated for once. I have the sides pulled back, secured with a beaded barrette, while my curls fall down my back.

The gang is all there. Deadeye and Ace wave us over. Everyone is sitting around several tables that they have pulled together. The men all stand as we arrive. Lots of back slapping and cheek kissing occur before we settle down into our seats. A waitress heads our way to get our drink order.

My health seems to be taking a turn for the worse over the last several days. Fatigue and nausea have become constant companions. I have had two nosebleeds this week as well as dizziness. Perhaps it is something left over from my injuries, but I can't be sure. It's been hard keeping all of this from Hawk. He worries so much with the nightmares and flashbacks. I should have gone easy at supper, but I lost my breakfast and lunch today, so I was starving and ate more than I should. It's going to come back up. Perhaps I should go to the clinic for a checkup.

"Charlotte, you look amazing tonight. I'm so glad you and Hawk could join us." Caroline says to me as we sit down.

"Thanks, Caroline. We are looking forward to visiting with everyone." I reply trying to be chipper than I feel.

"What can I get you to drink?" The waitress asks.

"Beer, Budweiser." Hawk says and looks to me. "A glass of red?"

"No, just water, I think. I'm not feeling alcohol tonight." I smile, afraid he will question me again. He has been worried over my nausea. I don't want him to be worried tonight. We just need to relax and have a little fun for once.

"Are you sick again?" Hawk asks me quietly where no one else can hear.

"A little." I reply honestly. I don't want to lie to him, but by not telling him all my symptoms, I suppose I am lying by omission. As I contemplate this thought, a sigh escapes my lips. I need to figure out what is going on with me, but it will have to wait for another time.

Tonight, we are going to enjoy our time with friends. Nothing is going to ruin this for us. I manage to swallow the bile that is rising in my throat.

After a couple hours of enjoyable conversation, Hawk leans into me and asks me to dance with him. I raise an eyebrow at him. We haven't ever danced before. I am not a good dancer and I certainly don't want to reveal my ineptitude in front of all our friends.

"Come on, love. I want you to dance with me." Hawk takes my hand and leads me out onto the dance floor. A new song comes on as we reach the center. Cole Swindell's, *Making My Way to You* begins to play. Hawk puts his arms around my waist, and I slide my arms around his neck. He pulls me in close and puts his mouth to my ear and begins to sing the song to me. He sings about how everything in his life has led him to find his forever, me.

By the time the song ends, I am in tears. Hawk pulls back from me and gets down on one knee. He pulls a box from his pocket and looks up at me expectantly as he opens the box.

"Charlotte, I know we haven't known each other very long. But like you said, we aren't children and we don't have a promise of tomorrow. Will you be my wife, my forever?" Hawk asks me.

"Yes!" I whisper. Barely able to get the words out around the huge lump in my throat and tears in my eyes. I am in shock. I never thought he was ready for this. I must be holding my breath because I am suddenly weak and lightheaded. As I faulter on my feet, Hawk sweeps me into his arms swinging us around in a circle. Cheers erupt from our tables. The whole bar is clapping for us. Hawk takes the ring from the box and places it on my ring finger on my left hand. It is the most beautiful ring I have ever seen. A large princess cut diamond on a white gold band with smaller diamonds on each side of the set.

When we return to the table, everyone is abuzz with congratulations and wanting to see the ring. This is complete heaven. I try not to think about what this means as far as my kids, my job, and my life goes. We have a lot to figure out, but right now none of that matters. We are just going to bask in the glow of the moment.

A little later, I head to the bathroom with Caroline, Summer, and Jessyka. I know why they never let anyone go alone, but I really don't want company at the moment. I am feeling sick again. Really sick and I know I am going to lose my supper when I reach the bathroom. As soon as we enter the restroom, I run for an empty stall. Once my stomach is emptied, I remain on my knees for several minutes. I am so weak. I just need a minute to get my strength back. If I didn't know better, I would think I was pregnant. I mean my boobs have been overly sensitive, the nausea, dizziness, and fatigue. Surely, I'm not, but we haven't used protection. Shit! I never even thought about it until this moment. I am a grown woman. I know how babies are made, but at my age I didn't really expect it. I should have been more responsible. It had been so long since that was even a concern. A soft knock on the door brings me back to reality.

"Charlotte, are you alright?" Jess asks me, quietly.

"Yes, I'll be out in a minute." I struggle to get my feet under me. I have to talk to Hawk. What will he say? He said he wanted us to have kids, right? Will he be upset with me? Is it too soon? He was there, too. I'm not the only one that was irresponsible. Sitting here in the floor, isn't going to change anything. It's disgusting actually.

Finally, I manage to get up and head for the sinks to wash my hands and the foul taste out of my mouth.

"You look like shit! Are you sure you are ok?" Summer, Jess, and Caroline are looking at me with concern. "You are so pale."

I try to put a smile on my face as I wash my hands and rinse my mouth. The water brings more nausea and I am again in the stall dry heaving for several minutes. When I emerge again from the stall on shaky legs, Jess puts her arm around my waist supporting me and Caroline gets on the other side. We leave the bathroom as a group. Wolf and Mozart are waiting for us in the hall. Hawk rushes across the room as he sees us emerge from the hall. I know I look a mess. I am pale, a thin sheen of sweat on my brow, and I am almost too weak to walk.

"Charlotte! What's wrong, love? Do you need to go to the hospital? Deadeye get my truck!" Hawk shouts as he pitches his keys to Deadeye.

"Hawk, I'm fine. I just need to lay down."

"You are not fine! I'm taking you to the hospital right now." Hawk says with determination.

"I don't need the hospital. I will go to the clinic tomorrow. It's not an emergency." I say to placate him.

"How can you say that? You are sick." Hawk continues to look at me with concern and fear.

"She's not sick, Hawk. If it's what I think, she will be fine, but she needs to rest." Jess says with a coy smile. I look at her and instantly know she is thinking the same thing I am as I nod at her.

Hawk looks back and forth between us frowning. He seems to decide something and nods. He sweeps me off my feet and heads for the door. As we leave the bar, Deadeye pulls up to the door with Hawk's truck. Hawk places me gently in the passenger seat, buckles my seat belt, and then rounds the truck to slide into the driver's seat that was just vacated by Deadeye.

"Should we call ahead to the ER, let them know you're coming?" Deadeye asks.

"No. We aren't going. I think we have somethings to talk about at home." Hawk replies quietly as he climbs in and put the truck in gear.

The ride home was in silence as I contemplated how I was going to tell him. We pull into the drive. Hawk shuts off the engine and exits the truck. I wait for him to open my door. He doesn't give me a chance to try to walk. He picks me up and carries me to the front door. Once inside, the alarm reset, and the doors locked. Hawk carries me through the bedroom and into the bathroom. He slowly undresses me, brushes my teeth, and washes my face. I don't even try to protest. This is something he needs to do. He needs to process what is happening. We just got engaged and realize that I am carrying his child all in the same night. Once he is done, he carries me naked to the bed. He pulls the covers down and lays me on the bed. He covers me and places a lingering kiss on my forehead.

"I'll be right back, love." Hawk whispers to me as he turns to go back into the bathroom. He returns several minutes later. He too is naked as he slips under the covers on his side of the bed. Without saying a word, he reaches for me. I go to him willingly. He rolls over me, kissing me deeply, reverently. Okay, he knows, but still he doesn't say anything and neither do I. I don't want to ruin the moment.

Hawk proceeds to make love to me, like never before. He is so tender, gentle. He kisses me from jaw to breasts. He suckles each nipple, nipping, licking, and teasing. He continues down my body leaving a trail of licks and kisses. Once he reaches my navel, he pauses. He cups my lower abdomen with his hands. He raises his head to look into my eyes.

"This is where our baby lives for now?" He asks quietly. I have tears in my eyes. I feel so loved in this moment.

"Yes." I whisper. It is the only thing that makes sense. It explains all my symptoms. I am still reeling with the implications.

Hawk gently kisses my belly. He rubs his hands over it so reverently. He continues to lower himself between my legs. He kisses my mound, my inner thighs, and my lower lips. He slides his hands under my ass lifting my hips to give him access to my wet sex. Using his thumbs, he parts my lips and slips his tongue between them. He licks from bottom to top and circles my clit. I shiver. He begins to suck on my clit, nipping it with his teeth. I buck my hips to meet his mouth. I am a feverish mess of need and want. I am soaking wet for him. I pull on his hair. I need to feel him inside me.

"Patience, love. Let me love you, worship you. You are giving me the greatest gift. You are carrying my child. I want you to feel the ecstasy I feel when thinking about what you are doing for me." Hawk whispers to me from between my legs. He looks up into my eyes while making his powerful declaration. I shudder from his words, his breathe on my thighs, and from the emotions running through me.

"Ok." I whisper back and relax back into the mattress. Hawk continues his ministrations bringing me to climax in a short amount of time. He moves back up my body, kissing his way to join my lips again. I am so enthralled with this man. How did I get so lucky? I know I don't deserve him, but I am so thankful for him every day. I know that with him at my side, I can be a mom again, even at my age.

Later after we are both sated and content; I am cuddled up to his side. Hawk runs his hands down my hair. Our breathing is still labored, and the sheets are soaked with sweat. I have never been happier in my life. I look down at the ring on my finger and stifle a chuckle. I am glad he asked me before we figured out that I was pregnant. I might have thought that was the only reason he asked me.

"Are you ok with this, love." Hawk asks me quietly. "I should I have been more careful. I didn't even think to use a condom. I wanted to feel you on my skin. I didn't want a barrier between us, but I should have been responsible."

"Hawk, I should have thought of it. I am a nurse practitioner for God's sake! I counsel my patients to always be diligent to prevent an unwanted pregnancy and prevent STD's. But I didn't want a barrier either and while I am shocked. I can't say this is unwanted. We are a little old to be having a baby, but I am honored to carry your child. I love that we have made a new life. A little piece of you and me, will live on after we are gone."

Turning to face him the love in his eyes overwhelms me. I am drowning in it. No matter what comes our way we will be alright. We can do this, even though we will be in our 60's by the time this baby is in college.

"I love you, Charlotte Williams, soon to be Jackson." Hawk says with a grin.

I love you, Jordan Jackson." I smile at him as I snuggle into his bare, hairy chest. I inhale his scent deeply. In minutes I'm asleep, content in the happiness that is my life. In the early morning hours wakefulness comes along with nausea so I run for the bathroom. In the bathroom on my knees at the toilet Hawk comes into the room and rushes to my side.

"Oh love, Are you ok? What can I do for you?" Hawk asks as he lifts me into his arms. He carries me to the bed and disappears into the bathroom. He returns a few seconds later with a cool wet cloth to place on my head. "I'm so sorry you are so sick. Is this normal? Were you this sick with your children?"

"No. I was never this sick, but each pregnancy is different." I say in contemplation. "I hope it doesn't last long. I'm just now physically getting over what happened in Columbia."

Later on, that morning, we go to the clinic and confirm that yes, I am pregnant with a blood test. They give me prenatal vitamins, something for nausea, and an appointment with an OB/GYN for next week. Hawk is beaming when we leave the clinic. He wants to call and tell everyone, but I convince him to wait until we see the OB next week.

A week passes so fast. We meet the OB, Dr. Rebecca Martin. She is very kind. We quickly explain our situation. I wasn't sure when my last period was, but Hawk remembers. He tells the doctor I was ending it when he found me, around August 18th. She examines me and checks some labs. Dr Martin decides that she wants to get an ultrasound. She thinks I am farther along than my dates. There is no way. I have not been with anyone except Hawk. She looks at me with sympathy. She thinks that I really was raped but blocked it out. Could that be possible?

She gets the equipment ready and begins the exam. I am looking at the screen, but I can't make heads or tails out of what we are seeing. It looks like there are two little peanuts, but she must have it on a split screen or something. Dr Martin begins to chuckle.

"Well that explains a lot." She says with a huge grin. She continues to move the wand and push buttons on the machine.

"What is it? Is something wrong?" I am in a near panic. Hawk is clutching my hand tightly. My eyes fill with tears.

"Oh, nothing is wrong." Dr. Martin says still laughing softly. "You are having twins, that's why you feel further along. It's also why your symptoms have been so bad."

What? We are having twins, really? I turn to Hawk. He looks as shocked as I am. I turn back to the screen and see 2 tiny heart beats moving in time to one another. When our eyes meet, a huge grin slowly spreads across his face. His eyes light up. He places a gentle kiss on my forehead.

"Thank you, love." He whispers to me. As I frown at him in confusion, he continues. "You are giving me two blessings. It's amazing. I was thrilled we were having a baby. I wanted us to have children, pleural, together, but I know we really didn't have the time with our ages. Here you are taking care of the problem. We are going to have them all at one time." He begins to laugh. I am quite certain he has lost his mind.

Dr Martin assures us that everything is fine. I voice concerns over my age, but she again tells us while we are at a higher risk for complications, not to worry. We ask about flying. I need to go see my children and meet Hawk's son. She says that will be fine up until the last trimester. She recommends that I take it easy and only work a part-time job at the most. Hawk declares that I won't be working at all if he has any say in the matter. Dr Martin sets us up for a follow up appointment in four weeks. He gets on the phone as soon as we are in the truck.

"Deadeye? Get the guys together, Wolf's SEAL team, call Olson, too and meet me at our house at 19:00 hours." Hawk says into the phone. "I have an announcement to make." After a pause, he continues. "It's even better than the engagement." He declares with a wink in my direction. I roll my eyes with a grin. He is going to be over the top over this pregnancy, but I am loving it.

CHAPTER 23

HAWK

WE HEAD to a department store and load up on supplies for an epic party. It's impossible to keep the grin off my face as we go through the store. Once we have gotten the cart full. We head to the check out. While standing in line, I can't keep my hands from Charlotte. The need to touch her is a compulsion. My hands wonder over her hips, up her back to her hair. Her hair smells like coconuts and reminds me of her in bed under me calling my name as I take her. People are beginning to stare. Charlotte is giggling like a schoolgirl with her first crush at my attention. I hear someone calling her name.

"Charlotte, Hawk what are you two doing today?" I look back into the store and see Summer, Jess, and Fiona coming up the aisle toward us. Charlotte looks to me as if she is unsure what to say. I just smile at her as I whisper in her ear while placing a kiss on her temple. "I've got this, babe."

"Hello, ladies." I say. "What are you up to today?"

"Shopping, but we asked you first." Summer replies, with an eyebrow raised in question and a coy smile on her face. The others are looking at us with similar expressions.

"We are shopping as well. We are having a little get together at our house on base tonight. Deadeye is supposed to be calling everyone to invite you." I inform the group. "I hope you all can make it."

"What's the occasion? I thought the engagement party was last week." Jess asks, grinning at me. She knows what is going on.

"Do we need to have a reason?" I ask with a smile. Jessyka knows our little secret or a least a part of it, but I have a feeling she hasn't disclosed it to anyone. "We had to leave so suddenly last time, I thought we might finish the party tonight."

"That's right! Are you feeling alright, Charlotte?" Fiona asks, her brow furrowed in concern.

"Yes, I am fine. Thanks for asking." Charlotte replies as she sways in my embrace. She must be dizzy again. I can't help but worry about the symptoms even though the doctor said everything was fine.

"Well, ladies it seems the line is moving. We will see you all this evening." I say in an almost sing-song voice. It is impossible to hide my good mood. We turn and head to the checkout counter.

A few hours later we are almost ready for our guests. Charlotte has been really sick today and very tired. She laid down as soon as we got home and has had a 2-hour nap. When she woke, I had almost everything ready for gathering. Streamers in neutral pastel colors, yellow, green, and purple along with several balloons have been placed around the house. Deadeye and Ace are here already. They are outside manning the grill. The food smells delicious. Charlotte seems to be avoiding being around the food. Nausea has kept her in the bathroom even more today. This pregnancy is going to be harder for her than either of her other pregnancies. It concerns me, but she has reassured me not to worry that it is common for a woman with twins to have strong symptoms.

A little while later, everyone else begins to arrive. Charlotte is pale and weak, but still gorgeous in my eyes. I want her to be the center of attention and feel like a Queen, because she is my Queen.

The house is filling with laughter, music, and friends. Several people ask what's up with the decorations? After all its Fall of the year and the place looks decorated for Spring (or a baby shower). I just smile politely and say we just like the colors. Which is true, not a lie. At least until we find out if they are boys or girls or one of each. I still can't believe this is happening. We are having twins!

Once we everyone has eaten, it's time to announce our secret. Charlotte is sitting in a chair in the living room. Lifting her easily I take her seat and sit her in my lap. I clear my throat loudly, but it's hard to get everyone's attention. Straw sees my struggle and whistles loudly. All eyes turn toward us.

"Charlotte and I invited you all to come here this evening to let you all in on a little secret." I declare with a huge smile. "We found out today we are going to be parents." I pause for dramatic effect. "of twins."

A loud chorus of congratulations, hoots, and hollers fills the room. I am so happy to overflow. I wasn't sure everyone would be as happy as we were, after all we haven't known each other that long. But in the long run it only matters what Charlotte and I think. We haven't told our other children yet. We really want to do that in person. Captain Olson has approved my leave to take Charlotte home to Kentucky to see her children. We will be leaving in a couple of day. After spending a little time with her kids, we are going to North Carolina to see my family.

A few days later we are landing at Fort Campbell, Kentucky. Captain Olson arranged for us to fly on a military transport instead of commercial. We are still concerned about Lopez looking for Charlotte. It will be harder for him to track her movements by not using commercial. Sara and Justin are here to pick us up and make the trek across Southern Kentucky to Charlotte's hometown of Deer Run.

Charlotte has been telling me all about her little town. It's more or less a dot on the map according to her. It's very rural with only a couple of gas stations, one grocery store, a bank, and few small general stores. There is a critical access hospital where she worked before her ill-fated trip. The population is only about five thousand for the whole county and about a thousand in the little town. Charlotte says everyone knows everyone. It's hard to keep a secret. I'm looking forward to getting a glimpse into her world that has made her the amazing woman she is today.

Once we disembark the plane, Sara and Justin are standing near the hanger. Charlotte starts to run to them, but I hold back gently. She looks at me with curiosity. She arches her eyebrows and I can't hold back a smile. She is so damn cute when she looks at me like that, half-pissed, half-curious.

"You're carrying twins, love. You shouldn't be running." I remind her gently as I pull her into my side. I can't hide the smile on my face as I think about the amazing precious cargo she carries in her belly. It's so hard not to be overprotective and dominating. It's because I love her and the babies, but I have to remember not to smoother her.

"Mom!" Sara and Justin run across the tarmac. We wait patiently for them to reach us. They swallow Charlotte in their embrace. I step aside to give them some space but can't stop smiling broadly. Charlotte's face is lit up in happiness. Her hazel eyes are sparkling with unshed tears. It's been hard for her to be so far from them and I momentarily feel guilty for taking so long to bring her home. It was in her best interest as it was just too dangerous before. Her countenance shifts as worry crosses her face but is gone in a flash. What is worrying her? It's what her children will think about our situation and all the changes and challenges we will be facing in the next year. It is a little overwhelming when you think about it. Getting married, having twins, blending two families that live so far apart. I'm stationed in North Carolina and her family lives here in Kentucky. It will all work out there is no other acceptable outcome other than Charlotte and I being together. She is the air I breath. I crave her more than any addict could a drug. I am startled out of my musing when Sara shrieks.

"Whoa, Mom What the hell? Where did that come from?" Sara exclaims grabbing Charlotte's left hand to look at the beautiful ring on her finger. "When were you going to tell us?"

"Now." Charlotte says softly. "I wanted to tell you in person. It's only been a little over a week. Please don't be angry. We wanted to be with you when we told y'all about it." Silently I move to her side, taking her hand, lending a silent support.

"Mom, we aren't angry, just shocked. I didn't realize you two were getting so close. It's really fast. Don't you think?" Justin inquires in a quiet voice.

"How about we wait to discuss all this until we are back at your place?" I interject wanting to take some of Charlotte's distress away at least for the moment.

"We can talk in the car. It's a long drive home." Sara says. Charlotte huffs out a breath and moves to head toward the parking lot. This is going to be a long awkward drive. Placing my hand on the small of her back, I gently guide her as we head to the parking lot. She is quiet and contemplative as we walk. I assume she is wondering what her kids are thinking. I really hope they take the news of the babies well. I won't stand for them upsetting her in her condition.

Justin insists on driving, so we settle into the back seat. Instinctively I reach over and buckle Charlotte's seatbelt as I have been doing since we arrived back in the States. It didn't cross my mind that her children might notice or even care. It's just something we always do. Sara turns to look over the seat at us, giving us a quizzical look. Charlotte glares back at her with a raised brow.

"What?" She demands.

"Are you suddenly helpless? He's buckling your seatbelt?" Sara smirks at us.

"Drop it Sara!" Charlotte reprimands in a tight voice. "I will not explain myself to you."

"Look, Mom. We haven't seen you in months except for a couple of days in the hospital. You haven't even talked about dating after Dad died. Now you are here sporting a huge rock. I am sorry, but this is all a bit much for us to take in, ok?" Sara's voice breaks with emotion at the end.

"I know. Ok? I am sorry. This hasn't been very easy for us either." Charlotte replies trying to placate them. "I realize Hawk and I have seemed to have moved too fast, but we are adults. We aren't young. We don't have endless time to build relationships. I would not presume to tell you how to live your life. I expect you not to try and tell me how to live mine."

"Charlotte, it is understandable they are surprised, and a little hurt. They want to protect you. They don't know me. Cut them a little slack." I say softly. I reach over to cup her cheek and sooth her anger. "Sara, Justin I want to reassure you that I only want what is in the best interest for your mother. I love her and I will never do anything to hurt her."

"Listen, we all need to calm down. I know this is an emotionally difficult situation, but we are family. Hawk is going to be a part of our family. I need you all to trust me that I know what I am doing." Charlotte tells her kids with tears in her eyes. This pregnancy has her crying nearly every day. She has assured me it was a normal thing, but it still hurts me to see her cry. The need to chase them away is ever present.

"We might as well completely clear the air while we are at it." Charlotte says with conviction. I stiffen beside her but squeeze her hand a little tighter in silent support.

"Charlotte, love, are you sure you want to do this now?" I asks her in a whisper.

"What's he talking about Mom?" Justin demands in a harsh voice as he flicks his eyes from the rearview mirror and back to the road. Fear flashes across her face as she contemplates their reaction to our news. She blows out a breath and chews on her bottom lip. The silence drags on, so I reach over and take her face in my hands. When her eyes meet mine, I ask her quietly. "Do you want me to tell them?"

"No. I will tell them." Charlotte declares as she takes a

deep breath. "Hawk and I are going to have twins in about 7 months."

The silence in the car is deafening. The roar of the tires on the road is a loud roar. Justin's knuckles are white on the steering wheel. Sara stares out the window. Charlotte is tense so I continue to hold her hand, gently rubbing my thumb over the back of her hand. I hate this. I don't want this to put a strain on our relationship. She looks to me and smiles sadly. When I slip my arm around her, she leans into me soaking up my strength. Before long she relaxes, and her breathing slows in sleep.

CHAPTER 24

CHARLOTTE

The gravels cracking under the weight of the tires wakes me we pull into the long driveway of my home place. A rabbit darts across the road into some dried bushes along the road. It is a beautiful old 2-story farmhouse. White vinyl siding, single oak front door, with large picture window gracing the front of the house. How I have missed this place. I bought it after my husband died. It was just too hard to stay there in our old house anymore, too many memories. Sara actually lives in the house where they grew up. Justin has moved about 40 miles away to be closer to his state police post.

We all pile out of the car. Justin helps Hawk get our bags and carry them into the house. Even though I slept on the four-hour drive here, I am exhausted after all the traveling. A nice long shower followed by a long nap is just what I need right now. Once we get inside, I am hit with nausea and dizziness again. I head for the downstairs bath. Hawk follows me. He knows that look. When we emerge from the bathroom, Sara and Justin are waiting outside giving us a hard look. I sigh heavily. Hawk pulls me to his side, pressing a kiss to my temple.

"Do you all need some time alone to talk?" Hawk asks.

"No." I say. "You are a part of me and therefore a part of this family."

"Look Mom. We just need some time to process all of this. We can't just accept some new random man. I am not saying that someday, we won't love Hawk like you do, but not today." It's Justin that drops all of the emotional words on us.

"Ok, I can understand that. Can you please try to understand that Hawk and I have been inseparable for the last few months? I need him. I'm sorry if that makes me seem weak in your eyes. I don't want you all to know all that I went through in the Columbian jungle. Hawk saved me in the jungle, and he continues to save me every day when I relieve that nightmare." I try to explain to them the closeness that Hawk and I have between us.

"Alright Mom, we get it. We will back off. I am glad that he is good to you." Sara says with a smile. "I'll run into town and get us something to eat for supper." We nod and Justin carries our bags upstairs to my room. I give Hawk a tour of the house and the back yard. A large deck graces the back of the house with a nice large grill and patio table and chairs. The backyard has a large fire pit with lawn chairs surrounding it. Benches, chairs, and small tables are placed strategically around the space. There is nothing we love more than inviting extended family over for barbeques.

Sara returns a short time later and we settle in around the dining table to eat. I am conscious to go easy on the greasy foods in hopes of keeping some of it down.

Hawk has been pushing water and Gatorade on me all afternoon. It's really sweet how he dotes on me. The need to be near him and touch him is overwhelming. I lay my hand on his thigh as we eat. His left hand takes mine on his lap. Thankfully the conversation is easy as the kids tell us about their jobs, recent dates, and outings they have taken with their friends. It's hard to stifle the yawn that escapes me as we are eating desert.

"I think it's time for you to sleep," Hawk declares as he places a kiss on my nose. He sweeps me off my feet and heads for the stairs. "Which room is yours?"

"Take a left at the top of the stairs. It's at the end of the hall." I laugh as he heads up the stairs.

"We are going to take off, Mom. We'll see you in the morning." Justin and Sara call.

Hawk carries me to the bed. He gently lowers me down. He climbs onto the bed with me. Instinctively I part my legs to allow him to kneel between them. He smiles wickedly. He knows what I want. It is getting to be an addiction. The need to feel him, feel his dick moving in and out bringing my body to a fevered pitch until I am screaming for more is an intense addiction.

"You should sleep, love. I'm sure the babies are tired, too." Hawk says even as he moves to kiss me. Reaching up and pulling him to me, I moan into his mouth as I move to deepen the kiss. I arch my chest so I can make contact with his.

"The babies can sleep even if I don't." I whisper. "I need you. I need you to make love to me."

Hawk smiles lovingly at me. He moves to make my dreams come true. His hands slide up my thighs. I shiver with need. He hands reach my panties and slides his hands inside. Ever so slowly he pulls my panties down my legs. He helps me to sit up while he lifts my dress up over my head and tosses it toward the floor. He reaches around me to undo my bra. He slides the straps down my arms and removes it freeing my breasts.

His breath hitches as he feasts his eyes on my chest. He reaches out to lovingly cup both breasts in his hands. My nipples harden, beading at his touch. He massages them gently. Suddenly, his mouth has descended to my left breast. He sucks gently at first, then fiercely, like his life depends on it. His teeth nip my nipple causing it to harden even more. He continues to bring me to life. I am in heaven as he loves my body.

When he comes up for air, I grab his face and kiss him deeply.

"You need to be naked." I say laughingly. "I need to feel your skin."

"God you are so damn sexy, love. I love it when you are so demanding." Hawk says.

"Then I am going to blow you mind, soldier boy." I say with a smirk. "Get. Naked. Now! I want you inside me, filling me, stretching me, making me come, hard."

"Damn, Wildcat! I love it when you talk dirty. I will fill your every fantasy." Hawk declares as he begins to remove his clothes. He sheds his jacket, followed by his t-shirt. He jumps up off the bed and quickly unbuttons his jeans slipping them along with his boxer-briefs to the floor. He slips off his shoes and steps out of his pants. Then he is over me. He spreads my thighs and lowers his head to kiss each thigh. He moves his mouth to my sex. He takes his hands and spread my folds. He leans closer and inhales deeply.

"You smell too good. I love your scent. It screams of your need for me. You are so wet. I could take you now, slide my dick in easily, soaking it in your heat." Hawk teases me. I am arching my hips toward him, moaning with my need for his hands, mouth, dick.

"Please Hawk, don't make me wait. Give me what I need." I beg him as he continues to stare at my pussy. "I need you, please don't make me beg."

"I will give you everything you need, baby. I want to take my time give you every pleasure." Hawk says with conviction.

"Can we do down and dirty first, then the slow and leisurely?" I inquire. I reach down to grip his long luscious length. I begin to pump it gently. Sliding my hands over his soft silky skin. I swirl my index finger over the head, slowly. I trace the slit in the center. I cup his balls with my other hand and gently squeeze. He sucks in a ragged breath.

"Love, I can't say no to you. Even when my way is better." He smirks at me. I raise up into a sitting position and move to kneel in front of him. I still have his shaft in my hand. I lean down and lick the tip of his dick, tasting his salty precum.

"Umm." I moan as I take his length into my mouth. He is sitting so still. I raise my eyes to look at him. His eyes are half closed. I smile around his shaft as I take even more in, I feel his head bump against the back of my throat. He moans when I begin to suck as I draw my mouth back up his length. I swirl my tongue along the underside. Once I reach the tip, I lick across it again. I lower my head again as I take him in, sucking hard.

Hawk moans and shudders as I continue my ministrations. He runs his fingers through my hair, gripping my head. I work him harder, faster, taking as much as I can trying to swallow him down. I feel him throbbing in my mouth.

"Stop, baby. I can't take much more. I want to come

inside you." Hawk says as he pulls my head away from his rock-hard length. A resounding pop echoes in the room as I break suction. I raise up to meet his gaze. His eyes are full of desire. He pushes me back onto the mattress. I am gasping for breath. He rolls me onto my stomach. He raises my hips and slips inside me. God it feels so good. I moan my approval. He begins to move, hard, fast, and deep. I love him so much and I love how he makes my body feel.

Sometime later when we are both sated, I sleep wrapped in his warm embrace. We make it the entire night without me waking from a nightmare. We are awakened the next morning to Sara clearing her throat at the door of the bedroom. We didn't think to close the door since we were alone in the house when we came in here. I turn to raise up and realize that the cover has slipped down to our waists and I am naked. A full-on blush floods my face as I snatch the sheet to cover myself.

"Um, Justin and I are back, Mom. I'm sorry to wake you." Sara stutters from the door. I realize our clothes are scattered haphazardly around the room.

"It's ok Sara. I sleep later these days. These little guys take a lot out of me." I say as I place my hand on my lower stomach. "We will be down in a little bit. We need to shower." I again blush profusely. It's way to awkward to have my daughter standing at the door of my bedroom where just a short time ago, I was having unbridled, passionate sex with my intended.

Sara smiles broadly. "Mom, we are all adults. I know how babies are made." Sara rolls her eyes and turns to head back downstairs.

After a nice leisurely shower, we descend the stairs to find not only Sara and Justin, but also my co-workers,

JoAnn, Lisa, and Dr Jones. I am floored. How did they find out I am here? We enter the family room. Hawk leads me to a recliner where he proceeds to steak his claim on me by sitting me in his lap.

"How are you all here? Who told you Charlotte was coming to town?" Hawk demands once we are comfortably seated. I stiffen waiting for the shouting to begin. Hawk is not at all happy.

"I convinced Sara and Justin to let us know when you would be coming home, Charlotte." Dr Jones announces. "We are very concerned about you. I don't understand why the military has insisted on keeping you captive in California."

"I have not been held captive by the military." I huff at Dr. Jones then turn my attention to my kids. "Sara! Justin! How could you betray my confidence? Do you all not understand how serious this is? I have a crazy, sex trader, gun running, drug lord who wants to drag me back to the Columbian jungle to beat and rape me. Why would you do this?" I demand. My voice getting higher the longer I talk.

"Mom I'm sorry, but these are your closest friends. I didn't think it would hurt to let them know you were here. They wouldn't betray your trust." It's Sara that answers. Justin just looks down at his hands.

"We would never hurt you Charlotte. You know us. Why have you let this man manipulate you? Has he brain washed you?" Dr Jones questions as he stands and takes a tentative step toward us.

"I would advise you to not go there." Hawk growls. He is tense and I can feel his anger brewing under the surface. I lean back into him. Place a kiss on his jaw and run my hand over his other cheek.

"Oh my God! Is that an engagement ring?" JoAnn

exclaims. All eyes in the room turn on us. Dr. Jones has a look of hurt, disappointment, and confusion on his face.

"Yes, it is. Hawk and I are getting married." I pause before continuing. "Dr Jones, no one has manipulated me. Hawk saved my life. No one was even looking for me. If him and his men had not raided the camp that day, I would still be in Columbia. I was beaten every day. I was violated." Dr. Jones looks horror stricken. "Lopez wants to take me back there. The fewer people who know where I am and where I am going the better. I don't think you would intentionally lead them to me, but if something slips… I can't go back there. I won't. I wouldn't live through it again." I am trembling. Hawk pulls me to him and rubs his hand up and down my back. With my head on his shoulder, I soak up his strength, his love.

"I don't want to be difficult, but you all need to leave. Charlotte is in no condition to be upset like this. I won't stand for it." Hawk says heatedly.

"What condition?" Lisa asks with concern. "Are you ill or still suffering from your injuries?" War is raging in my heart. I can't lie to my friend, but should I reveal my pregnancy? Justin decides for me.

"Mom's expecting." Justin informs the room. Several loud gasps are heard before Justin stands and gestures for everyone to head toward the door. Lisa stands and walks slowly toward us. Once she is close enough, I stand, and she reaches out to hug me. We cling to each other for a moment. I whisper to her I will call her and bring her up to speed. Dr Jones and JoAnn stand and slowly begin to make their way toward the door. I can't even look at them as they leave. Before they reach the door, JoAnn stops and turns. Hawk rises to his feet behind me, wrapping his arms protectively around my waist.

"How long will you be in town, Charlotte? I was hoping we could spend some time catching up while you are home. I seriously doubt the drug lord is even interested in you." JoAnn looks at me in anticipation.

"We aren't giving you our itinerary. It puts Charlotte in danger. So, stop asking." Hawk growls. He is livid. His arms are trembling around me. His posture is stiff, and his jaw is ticking rapidly.

"Oh, I'm sorry. I didn't mean any harm. It's really unnecessary for you to be so dramatic." JoAnn says sarcastically. "It's fine, just call me sometime, ok?"

"Sure." I say. I just want them to leave. I never realized how rude JoAnn was before. Or maybe I did, and I just chose to ignore her. With a sigh I lean on the man that will keep me safe against all cost. He pulls his phone out and sends off a text. After the guests have left, Hawk declares that we cannot stay here any longer. He goes up stairs and packs what little we have used since arriving. He comes back down with all our belongings. Justin and Sara look on in shock. I am a little stunned also.

"What? Where are you going?" Justin demands as Hawk takes my hand to lead me to the door.

"I am sorry Justin. We can't stay here knowing that other people might know. I will not put your mother's life, or our babies lives in danger." Hawk says as he turns toward the door. "We will be back in a few days. Once I am sure that there is no longer any danger to Charlotte or the twins."

Hawk leads me out the door. I am not sure where we are going, but when we emerge there is a large SUV sitting in the driveway. Hawk leads me to the passenger side and settles me in the back seat, buckling my seat belt as he sides in beside me.

"I have contacted your parents for you, Hawk. No one knows where we are going." The man driving says once we are in our seats and the door is shut. He is already backing out of the driveway. I have no idea where we are going, but as long as I am with Hawk, I am not afraid.

CHAPTER 25

I CANNOT BELIEVE this is really happening. Her stupid friends are going to get her fucking killed if I am not careful. I must keep Charlotte safe at all costs. It's not only the fact that she is carrying my children. It's that I need her in my life. She has in a short amount of time become my life, my everything. I can't live one day of my life without her in it.

I want to kick her so called friends asses. They are so naive that they don't see the danger she is in at the hands of the madman. If I didn't know any better, I would think one of them wanted something to happen to her. I don't like the way that Dr Jones looks at her. I know that look. It's the same one I see in the mirror when I think about Charlotte. The way she looks soaked in sweat with her lips swollen from our love making. She is glorious and I love this woman. He has feelings for her, too, but she doesn't feel the same about him. If he tries to do anything to come between us, he will regret it.

Charlotte is so astounding under these circumstances. My heart is full of pride in her and her strength.

She didn't complain or resist when I packed our bags and walked us out of her house and away from her kids. It makes my dick hard thinking about how much she trusts me. I have never had a woman to trust me so completely. She has been taking care of herself for the last five years, but she is willing to let go of some of that control to let me care for her. It's as if she knows how much I need to take care of her.

After a very long drive we reach my parent's house. My son, Brian is already here. He stalks out of the house with a scowl on his face. I open the door and slide out of the hummer as I reach in to get Charlotte. I help her to the ground, by letting her body slide down mine. I place a kiss to her forehead as her feet settle on the ground. She is so damn cute. She looks divine. Her hair is a mess where I have been running my fingers through it.

"Hello, son." I say as he rounds the front of the SUV. He comes up to me and hugs me hard slapping my back. He makes me proud. He is really growing into a strong young man. He is my height now. He is getting strong broad shoulders. His black hair is getting wavy. He has let it get longer than I would like for it to be.

"Dad! I am glad you are here." Brian declares, smiling broadly as he pulls back from me. "This your lady friend?"

"Brian, I would like you to meet Charlotte Williams."

"Hello, Charlotte. It's nice to finally meet you in person. It's just not the same on Facetime. You are more beautiful in person." Brian extends his hand out to take Charlotte's. Pride blooms in my chest as he places a kiss on the back of her hand. I have taught him well. He is going to be a good man someday soon.

"Hi, Brian. I'm glad to meet you, too." Charlotte says as she reaches out tentatively to pull Brian into a hug. He hugs her back. This makes me happy to see them together and getting along. Brian knew that I was asking Charlotte to marry me, but not about the news of the twins. That's a topic for after we eat. Besides I only want to tell it once. It's better to wait until we are with Mom and Dad, too.

"I want to see the ring. Dad sent me a picture, but I want to see it in person." Brian says as he reaches to grab her left hand. Brian oohs and awes over the ring. He can always make me smile even when I am stressed and worried. "So, have you set a date yet?"

"Not yet. How about we head inside? No need to be hanging out in the driveway." I say and begin to lead Charlotte to the house. Scanning our surroundings there is no sign that anyone is about or watching us.

The house is a nice 2-story log cabin nestled in a copse of trees about 2 miles off the main road. Deadeye and the rest of the team will be here by mid-night. As soon as I knew about the breach in Charlotte's security, I called Captain Olson while I packed our things. He had the guys rounded up and heading this way even before I hung up the phone.

Charlotte steps up onto the large wrap around porch and into the foyer of the house. The foyer has shiny, mahogany wood floors. The steps that lead to the upstairs set off to the right just past the door to the large family room. The family room is littered with furniture, mostly cream-colored couches, recliners, and padded benches. A large flat screen TV hangs on the far wall over the fireplace. Light streaming in the large picture window cast a warm glow on the room. Mom and dad love to entertain family and friends.

The smell of roast, vegetables, and cornbread fills the house. I catch a whiff of cinnamon also. Mom has filled the house with such wonderful smells. We continue on into the house toward the back. I turn Charlotte left and lead her into the dining room. A large cherry formal dining table is already set with plates, glasses, and silverware. Candles are lit on the table and the buffet table along the near wall, is already being laden with food. A large basket of browned rolls, a platter of roast and vegetables, and a plate of cornbread is already sitting on the buffet.

The door to the kitchen swings open and my mother busts through the door, casually dressed with her perfectly styled short dark brown hair. She has declared that she will never be grey no matter her age. She has a little extra weight around the middle and her skin is looking thinner than I remember. Even at 69 years old she still gets around as well as women a half of her age. She is carrying a plate of cinnamon rolls for dessert. She knows they are my favorite. She always makes them when I come home.

Dad follows her out the door carrying a bottle of wine and chuckling at something my mother has said. Dad is 6'1" with salt and pepper hair that he still wears in a military cut. Despite his age of 72 he is still fairly muscular and can keep pace with Brian, my brothers, and myself. His shoulders are broad, and his biceps still bulge under his dress shirt. I hope I will age as well as he has. They spy us and my mother hurries to set down the plate she is carrying.

"Jordan, your home at last!" Mom hurries to embrace me, ruffling my hair. Mom is about 5'2" so her head barely reaches the middle of my chest. Dad comes over and claps me on the back.

"It's good to have you home son." Dad says.

"It's good to be home." I say to Dad as I return their

hugs. "Thanks for putting us up on such short notice. Everything smells so wonderful, Mom. You always out do yourself." I look around to see Charlotte standing off to the side looking a little awkward. I reach for her and pull her to my side. I wrap my arm around her waist and kiss her gently on the temple.

"Mom, Dad this is Charlotte. My soon to be wife." I inform them. She is nervous. She is standing so stiffly in my embrace. She trembles. "Charlotte this is my Mom, Diane and My Dad, Jordan, Sr." Mom instantly pulls Charlotte into her arms and places a big kiss on her cheek. Charlotte visibly relaxes at the warm welcome from mom.

"Charlotte, it's so wonderful to meet you in person at last. I couldn't wait to meet the woman that has stolen Jordan's heart. My son doesn't bring women home to meet the family. I knew you were special when he asked about bringing you here." My mother rattles on. Dad takes Charlotte's hand in his and kisses the back of her hand. "It's wonderful to finally meet you, Charlotte." My dad tells her. "Jordan has been keeping us updated on your recovery. We are overjoyed about the engagement. It's past time he found him a good woman to take care of him." Dad chuckles as he finishes.

"I'm happy to meet you, too." Charlotte replies quietly. She has talked to both of them on Facetime, but I know it's different for her meeting my parents for the first time. Brian enters the dining room after having taken our bags upstairs to our room. "Is it time to eat? I'm starving!" Brian declares as he pulls out a chair at the table and plops down.

"Oh yes, it is!" Mom replies. "I was just standing here, talking away. I don't where my manors are at. I'm sure you must be hungry after traveling so much. Have a seat and let's eat."

Dad takes his place at the head of the table, while Mom sits to his right. I take Charlotte around the table and pull out the chair in the middle of the table. Once she is seated, I take the chair to her right which is the seat on Dad's left. After Dad says grace, we all dig in and enjoy a leisurely meal. Once we have all eaten our fill, Mom suggests we move to the family room to have coffee and cinnamon rolls for dessert.

We head into the family room. I sit in one of two recliners and pull Charlotte into my lap. She sits stiffly and I realize she is uncomfortable with the intimacy in front of my parents. My Dad has taken the other recliner, while Brian has stretched out on the sofa. Mom is last to arrive as she is bringing in the tray with coffee and rolls. After Mom has gotten everyone coffee and rolls, she moves to sit in my Dad's lap. Charlotte relaxes then. I stifle a chuckle. She looks at me with curiosity. She hadn't noticed that she was being tense.

"So, Jordan tell me as much as you can about what is going on that has brought you to our remote location." Dad inquires as Brian turns on the TV and begins to flip through the channels.

"Well like I have told you Charlotte overheard some important information by some seriously bad men." I begin. "We have kept her on base and out of the press in an effort to prevent them from knowing where she is staying. But it has been several weeks, and the chatter has died down. So, I brought Charlotte to Kentucky to visit with her children. They didn't fully comprehend the danger that she is in at the hands of this madman. They told some of her co-workers and they showed up at her home. I had a bad feeling that it would be leaked to the press and she would be in danger of being harmed again. I just needed to get her away from there before something happened."

"I just don't understand why people have to be so evil." Mom states, "Why would anyone want to hurt such a beautiful, sweet woman? I've only been around you for an hour and I already can tell you are a kind, caring person. It just boggles my mind."

"Mom it isn't because Charlotte is or isn't a kind person. It's because she helped to thwart the kidnapping of members of border patrol agents' family members. The drug lord had planned to use the kidnap victims to force the agents to allow drugs, weapons, and sex slaves across the border." I tell Mom. She always sees the best in people. It's hard for her to accept that some people are just evil.

"Son, you know you and Charlotte are welcome here anytime and for as long as you need." Dad declares.

"Thanks, Dad and Mom. I appreciate it." I say quietly as I contemplate how to approach the subject of the twins.

"Brian did you put their things in your Dad's old room?" Mom asks.

"Yes, I did." Brain announces. He is still running through the channels on the TV.

Charlotte yawns quietly. She tries to hide it behind her hand, but I know she is tired despite us have had a nap earlier in the day on the way here. I should get her to bed. She has been so tired in recent weeks. I had been worried about her fatigue. I didn't know if something was medically wrong or if she was sinking into depression. Of course, now I know it's because of the babies growing inside her. I want to tell my family even though I am not sure how they will react.

"Jordan, have you and Charlotte set a date for the wedding yet?" Mom asks. She has her right eyebrow raised in question with anticipation on her face.

"No, we haven't, but it will be soon. I don't want to wait. I never know when I am going to be called up to leave on a mission. Also, we have some news that will inevitably move up the date." I announce. I feel Charlotte tense straightening her spine. She sits up in my lap. I miss her warmth. She was snuggled in so nicely against my chest with her head on my left shoulder.

"News? What news?" Mom asks with a look of joy on her face. I know Mom will be happy about the babies. She has often scolded me for not finding a good woman and giving her more grandbabies.

"Well, we recently discovered that Charlotte is pregnant, and she is carrying twins." I let the news sink in, waiting for whatever the response will be.

"Twins!?" Echoes through the room as Mom, Dad, and Brian all register what I have said at the same time. Mom is suddenly on her feet and at our side. She embraces Charlotte and I in a giant hug. Dad comes over to shake my hand. I look to see what Brian's reaction will be. I don't think he will be upset, but you never know how teenagers will react.

Brian has sat up on the couch and is looking at us with an unreadable expression on his face. Once Mom and Dad have congratulated us, Charlotte gets to her feet and walks over to sit by Brian on the couch. She takes his left hand in her right one. She stares at him until he meets her gaze.

"Brian, I know this is all happening rather fast, but I hope you can be happy to be a brother. They will not be taking your place. We are just making this family a bit bigger. Your dad and I are going to need all the help we can get with these two. You know that he travels a lot because of his job. I am going to need a man around to help me when he is gone. I hope that will be you. Also, I have 2 grown children that I look forward to you meeting, soon. I hope you can come to think of them as your big brother and sister." Charlotte tells him all the while holding his hand and looking intently into his eyes.

"I never thought I would have siblings, even though I wanted them. Dad never dated and my Mom is never around." Brian says quietly. "It's a little overwhelming to be getting 4 at one time, but I am happy to be getting them. I am glad that you and Dad are together. He seems so happy now. I didn't realize how unhappy he had been until he met you and changed so much."

I move over to sit on Brian's other side and place an arm across his shoulders to give him a tight one arm hug. "I am happy, son. I didn't realize that I was unhappy either until I met this wonderful woman in an airport café. She turned my world upside down and walked away. I was kicking myself for not asking her name and phone number. Fortunately for me and unfortunately for her, she got caught up in a mess of trouble and I was able to be there to bring her out of it."

We all chuckle at that statement. After saying our goodnights, I take Charlotte by the hand and lead her up the stairs to our room for the night. She slips into the in-suite bathroom to get ready for bed. She emerges 15 minutes later dressed in a t-shirt and shorts. I enter the bathroom and quickly get ready for bed. I can't wait to get naked with her. I am so happy that our family knows about the twins and seem to be happy for us. It's time to celebrate. Once we are both settled in bed, Charlotte giggles. Soon her giggling has become a full-on belly laugh.

"What is so funny, love?" I question her. She struggles to gain enough control to talk. She has tears streaming from her eyes. Once she can finally speak, she tells me.

"I was so nervous and feeling embarrassed to be sleeping with you in your parents' house, with your son in the next room. Then I realized that I am knocked up with twins, it's a little late to be embarrassed. I mean they obviously know we've been having sex." Charlotte manages to squeak out between laughs.

Pondering on what she has just revealed, I too begin to laugh. I didn't realize she had been feeling insecure or embarrassed about having sex in my parents' house. Perhaps, I should have been the one to be embarrassed. I have never had a woman in their home, not even Julie. I have just become so comfortable with her that it never crossed my mind. Once I am over my laughter, I reach for her. Pulling her to my side and slip my hand under her t-shirt to rub her soft skin on her abdomen. She shivers under my touch. My hand slides up to cup her ample breasts. Her nipples harden at my embrace and her breath hitches.

"I don't want to make you uncomfortable, love. I can hold off until we are no longer under my parents' roof." I whisper in her ear to assure her I won't push her for sex while we are here.

"Seriously?" She questions me as she pulls back to look me in the eye. "You are rubbing on me and whispering in my ear all sexy and you tell me we will wait?" her voice rising higher as she continues to speak. "How long are we here for? 2-3 days? A week? Are you trying to kill me?"

Now I am crying with laughter. She looks so damn cute when she is pissed. I can't take her seriously. I am shaking all over trying not to laugh out loud. I have to look away, because the more she scowls at me, the funnier the whole situation seems.

"Are you laughing at me now? I can't believe you are getting me horny, leaving me hanging, and then laughing about it. You are being an insensitive jerk." She huffs out a breath blowing her hair back from her face. She then makes a big production of turning over to face away from me. Now she has made it worse. Everything she does is so fucking cute, I can't help but laugh. I get my composure back after a couple of minutes and I grab her a little forcefully as I settle her body next to mine. I press my erection into her back and grind against her.

"I'm sorry, love. I didn't mean to tease you. I swear you are so damn cute when you are mad. I just can't take you seriously when you are mad and huffing."

"Hawk, you are not helping your cause to get in my pants." Charlotte informs me. "I think we just need to sleep while in your parents' home."

"Alright, love. Whatever you want. I will respect that, but if you change your mind just say the word and I will have you fucked and satisfied in minutes."

"Oh God Hawk, you are going to be the death of me." Charlotte laughs as we settle into one another for the night. It's quite sometime later, before her breathing becomes slow and steady. I tighten my arms a little more around her. A few minutes later, I relax, and I am sleeping soundly.

CHAPTER 26

CHARLOTTE

HE'S HERE and he is coming for me. I hear the soft scuffling of boots on the ground. I hunker down behind a tree. I try to hold perfectly still. Maybe he can't find me if I don't move. Suddenly hands are grabbing at me. Pulling me up by my hair. His punches me repeatedly. I try to protect my abdomen. I can't let him hurt the babies. He growls in my ear.

"You will pay, bitch! I will take from you all that you have cost me, starting with your military man. How dare he think he can keep you from me? Yes, I know all about you, about your children, your man and his son. I know everything and I will get you. I have friends that will lead you back to me. I will kill him, your children, both born and unborn while I make you watch. Finally, I will kill you after you are no longer useful to me. You cost me men, money, and time. I will get my revenge. You will regret the day you interfered in my business."

I fight him. I kick and punch against him. I have to protect Hawk, our children, and the babies. I won't let this evil man take them away from me.

Jerking awake I am soaked in sweat, tears are streaming down my face, and I am shaking uncontrollably. I look around unsure at first where I am. Is this another flashback? Turning to my left, the bed is empty and the room is dark. There is no light coming from the window on my side of the bed. It must still be early morning. The room is a beautifully decorated bedroom. It's Hawk's room at his parents' house. I begin to relax as I realize I was having a nightmare. I am still unsettled several minutes later when Hawk enters the bedroom from the hallway. He takes one look at me, furrows his brow, and rapidly stalks to the bed. He climbs onto the bed and reaches for me.

"What's wrong Charlotte? You look like you've seen a ghost."

"I'm ok, Hawk. It was just a nightmare, but it seemed so real. It was nothing like the ones I have had before." A shudder shakes me as I remember Lopez's words in my dream. He means to hurt me and my family. I am certain of it, but how can I convince anyone that Lopez is coming for me and Hawk from a dream.

"I have changed my mind. I need you to take away my nightmare." I say seriously. Reaching out I take hold of his large biceps. Pushing him back onto the mattress, I climb up to straddle him. His hard length presses against my sex through the thin layers of material separating our bodies. Slowly grinding my pelvis over his erection, my core moistens at the thought of him entering me. My hands run over the expanse of his hairy chest. His nipples are hard and his pectoral muscles flex under my hands as he moves his arms to circle my waist.

He slips his hands under the hem of my t-shirt and slides them over my bare skin. I shiver at his touch in anticipation of what I know is coming. His erection throbbing under me. It is wanting to break free from his pajama bottoms and enter me, hard and deep. I press harder into his groin with mine. A moan/growl escapes his lips as he bucks his hips to match me. In moments, my shirt is gone. My shorts quickly follow along with Hawks bottoms. I again climb across him.

Raising my hips to give him room, he grasps his erection at the base and positions the head at my entrance. Slowly I slide down his length one inch at a time, until I feel his head hit my cervix and my groin is joined tightly with his. I pause letting him stretch me, basking in the fullness and feeling of completeness. It feels like we have become one person. Then I reverse just as slowly, just before I let the tip slip from my folds I slam back down hard. Hawk almost seems startled, but quickly matches me thrust for thrust as I rise and fall on him.

He reaches up and grasps my breasts, squeezing almost to the point of pain. It feels amazing. His hands on my breasts while his dick is buried deep inside me. As I quicken the pace, I feel the tension building in my core. He lowers a hand and gently swirls the tip of his index finger over my clit. He continues to increase the speed and pressure of his touch as I ride him. It doesn't take long until we are both coming hard, calling each other's names. I shudder over him as he stiffens pumping the last of his cum into me. I melt on top of him, fully sated and in need of sleep.

Hawks team has arrived by the time we come downstairs later that morning. Deadeye and Straw bring us up to date on the latest intel on Lopez and his gang. It appears that they have backed off and are laying low. He has been plagued with his competitors intercepting shipments and trying to take over some of his territories. Sources close to him report he has declared he isn't going to waste any more time or resources looking for the American woman. He has other problems at the moment. It brings me great comfort after the horrible dream I had early this morning.

We spend a couple of days at Hawk's parents' home. It is a pleasant relaxing time for us. I get to know his family better especially, Brian. He is a really sweet, intelligent young man. It's plain to see the influence Hawk and his parents have had on him. He is a gentleman despite being a teenage boy. He put my comfort ahead of his just like his father. We will have to head back soon. Hawk's leave will be up, and I am increasingly nervous about the day he will be forced to leave me for a mission.

I also meet Hawk's brothers, sisters-in-law, sister, brother-in-law, and nieces and nephews. It's a large family when they all get together. Hawk is the oldest. His brother, Jason is next oldest and is married to Jessica. Jason looks a lot like Hawk. He is tall about 6'2" with the same black hair. He is clean shaven and his has sharp chiseled jawlines. He is also very muscular. He is also a Marine. Neither he nor Hawk talk about what type of soldier he is.

His wife is a beautiful, sweet woman. Jessica is tall at 5'10". She has auburn brown wavy hair. She is thin, but muscular. I am slightly jealous, but don't really want to put in the time required at the gym to look like she does. She is a Marine, too, but she is on the reserves now. They have 2 small children. She wants to be home with them if possible. Their son Micah is 5. He has the black straight hair of the Jackson men. He is quite the inquisitive little man. He is full of questions, but I really enjoy playing with him. Their daughter Mila is 2. She is so cute with dark brown wavy hair. She talks non-stop and her vocabulary is fairly extensive for her age.

Hawk's sister, Danica is the third child of Diane and Jordan, Sr. She has her mother's brown hair, height, and build. She also has the same bubbly friendly personality. She is married to Markus. They have a baby boy, Michael. He is 8 months old and so full of energy. He is adorable crawling around on his chubby little legs and arms. His smile is radiant. I am in love when he crawls over to me and allows me to pick him up. I try reading him a baby book that he can chew on, but he has more fun flipping the pages. After a time, he lays his little head over on my breast and falls asleep. Danica enters the room and laughs when she sees Michael. "He loves breasts!" She laughs. Hawk embarrasses me by saying that I have nice large breasts that a guy can sleep on. Everyone laughs as my face turns nine shades of red.

Joseph is the youngest of the gang and is married to Ellen. Joe is 6'3" with dark brown hair. He is like Hawk with a full beard and mustache. It is kept neatly trimmed. He is also like his father and brothers; he is beautifully built. He is SWAT. He originally chose the Navy, but after meeting his wife he left the service once his tour was up and he joined the police force. Ellen is about my height at 5'4" with dark blonde wavy hair. She is sweet, friendly, and very capable. Joe seems a little overbearing much like his brothers, but she matches him to a tea. They have two girls, Maddie that is 7 and Morgan who is 4. They both have dark blonde hair like their mother, that falls in ringlets to their shoulders.

The house is chaos. Everyone is talking at the same time. It's a little difficult to keep up with the multiple conversations going on at the same time. Hawk's family was so welcoming. It wasn't long before I felt like I had known them forever. They told stories of their youth and the mischief the boys got into and about harassing all the boys that tried to date their sister. It was all in fun and I was sad when it was time to leave the safe abode.

We head back to my home the third day. A foreboding sense of unease seems to swallow me, but I don't voice my fears to Hawk, not wanting him to worry. I just want to enjoy the time we have left together before the real world comes knocking on the door. I call Sara and Justin to let them know we are back once we have gotten settled in. Deadeye and the others have headed back to base in California feeling confident the danger to my safety is over for now. Early the next morning, the ringing of Hawk's phone wakes us from sleep.

"Hawk here" Hawk answers the phone. He listens intently. He tenses next to me. His face falls and a frown forms on his brow. He reaches over and absently runs his fingers through my locks. An array of emotions pass across his face. They flash so quickly it was hard to register them all. Regret, anxiety, anger, frustration, anticipation, and love for me all cross his face as he listens to the caller on the other end of the line.

"Alright, I understand. I will be on the next flight out." Hawk tells the caller. He hangs up the phone and sighs heavily as his shoulders slump. He turns to me and rolls me onto my side and pulls my back to his front. He runs his hands up and down my arms and side. He blows out a deep breath. I am scared at the range of emotions, but I want to give him time to process what he has to tell me. After several minutes, he relents to tell me that our plans have changed.

"That was Captain Olson. We have been called up for a mission." Hawk drops the bomb I have felt coming for the last 24 hours. I hold my breath waiting to hear the rest. I know there won't be much. He cannot tell me anything where he is going, how long he will be gone, or what he will face while there. I must be strong for him. The last thing he needs is for me to fall apart. I won't have him worrying about me and our babies while he is fighting for the lives of himself and his teammates.

"I don't know how long I will be gone or even where we are going yet. I will get the details once we are back on base, but I still won't be able to tell you anything." Hawk sighs again. He keeps rubbing my arm and touching my hair. I know that I have to assure him I will be fine while he is gone. So, I turn in his embrace to face him.

"Hawk, I know you wanted us to have more time together, but I will be fine while you are gone. I know that you, Deadeye, Straw, Ace, Wallace, Tank, Worm, Hack, Virus, and Mercury are more than capable to taking care of yourselves no matter what you are sent to do. I will miss you, but I know you will come home to us. I love you so much it hurts sometimes. I can stay here while you are gone. I will split my time between here and your parents' home. Diane said I was welcome anytime. I will just take her up on her offer." I chuckle as I finish in an attempt to lighten the dark mood that has descended on us.

"Charlotte, I would be honored and feel better if you stayed with my parents. Dad is retired Navy and despite his age he stays in shape and keeps his skills up to pare, but I don't want you staying here alone. What if something happens while Sara and Justin aren't here? You could fall and hurt yourself or become ill and not be able to get to the phone to call for help. I am still uneasy about Lopez. It just seems bizarre to me that he would suddenly drop his revenge. I don't want to frighten you, but we have to be realistic."

"Hawk, I will do whatever you ask me to do. I trust you completely. I need to know that you aren't worrying about what is going on at home. I don't want you to be distracted and get hurt or killed on your mission. I need you. Our babies need you. And even though he acts like a grown man, Brian still needs you." I tell him as I slide closer to him to place a kiss on his lips. It is a hesitant kiss. I want to comfort him, reassure him of what he means to me, to our family.

Before I can register his intent. Hawk has rolled on top of me to consume me, body and soul. The kiss deepens and becomes sensual. I part my lips, letting him devour my mouth. His hands are moving over my naked body. I feel him harden between my legs and I arch my hips up to meet his groin. I moan in my lust and I hear him growl his need against my mouth. He breaks the kiss to move his mouth over my skin. I am lost in the moment. It feels like this is goodbye. A tear slips from my right eye, but I choke them back. I won't ruin this moment with tears.

Hawk proceeds to bring me to climax several times over the next hour. Finally, when my body feels like Jell-O at a picnic on the fourth of July, he carries me from the bed to the bathroom. He fills the garden tub with hot water and turns on the jets. He lowers me into the tub and climbs in behind me. We sit and soak in silence for a while, when the water begins to cool, he washes me and pulls the plug to drain the tub. He then transfers us to the shower to rinse the bubbles from our bath away. He towel dries me and wraps a towel around me. Sweeping me up into his arms he carries me back into the bedroom. He drops me on the bed and heads to the dresser and gets clothes out for me. He comes back to the bed still not saying a word he dresses me in comfort clothes for traveling. Then he dresses in his military fatigues and combat boots.

There is a knock at the door. Hawks face falls briefly,

but then he leans down to place a gentle kiss on my forehead, lingering just a little too long. Struggling to keep the tears from falling, I cling to his shoulders and breath in his scent deeply. I need to memorize every detail of him, his scent, his soul. He pulls back from me gently.

"I have to go now, love. They are here to take me back to Fort Campbell to catch a plane out back to base. Dad will be here in a couple of hours to take you home with him." Hawk looks into my eyes. His eyes roam over my face, then down my body. His hand comes to rest on my lower abdomen. "I love you, Charlotte. I love our babies. I want us to get married as soon as I get home. I wish we had done it while we were here. I will be back home for you as quickly as I possibly can."

"I know, Hawk. I love you too, soldier boy." I smile up at him with love in my eyes. I want him to leave with a happy memory, not with me sobbing like my world is ending. I manage to keep the tears from falling even as I feel them pooling in the corners. We hold onto one another like it's the last time we will be together. After a few moments, he pulls back and kisses me gently. He turns and walks out my room.

Hawk is gone. The tears are falling freely now, but I have to pull myself together and get ready. His Dad will be here in a few hours. My clothes are packed, and the suitcase is by the door in less than fifteen minutes. Now what do I do? My phone rings. It's an unfamiliar number.

"Hello?" I say into the phone.

"Charlotte, darling? This is Jordan, Sr. I am afraid I am going to be later than expected. I have a flat tire, but I'll be there as soon as I can. I can call Joe and see if he can come down sooner?" Jordan, Sr questions.

"No, Jordan. I will be fine. I'll just read a book or

something until you can get here. Don't worry about me. I may call my friend Lisa and chat with her for a while. Be safe and I'll see you soon."

"Alright. Charlotte?" Hawk's dad asks.

"Yes?"

"Stay put until I get there, ok? Don't answer the door for anyone or let anyone know you are there alone. I hope this whole drug lord mess is behind you, but we don't want to take chances. I'll be there soon, darling."

"I'll be fine, Jordan. I appreciate you worrying about me. I'll be waiting for you." I say as the connection ends.

I decide to call Lisa and catch her up on all that has happened since I was abducted in the jungle. We talk for a long time. I have missed her and our talks. She could always help me to process my emotions and help me find clarity when all I can see is haze. After updating her about the awful time I spent in captivity the conversation turns to my new relationship.

"Sooo…tell me about your man." Lisa demands with a laugh. "Don't get me wrong. I am thrilled for you. Your face lights up when you look at him. Don't get me started on the looks he gives you. They make me envious. I wish I had a man look at me with such love and devotion. Give me details about how all this came about."

"Honestly, I have no idea how I got so lucky. You remember me telling you about the soldiers in the café at the airport?" I ask.

"Yes. I remember. You talked to them while waiting for the rest of us to get to the airport before we headed off to Guatemala." Lisa replies.

"That's right. Jordan was the one that kissed my hand. When I woke up in the safe house and he was there, I couldn't believe it. I thought I was dreaming or hallucinating, but he was there." I sigh as I recall the intense conversations we shared while waiting for me to be well enough to travel. "He remembered me from the café, too. He confessed he had been thinking about me too since we first met. He refused to leave my side while we were at the safe house. I was a stranger, but he cared for me like I was already his wife. Hell, better than I had ever been treated before.

"You know that I loved David, but he was not really the alpha male type like Jordan is. When Jordan gets it in his head that I need something, there is no changing his mind. He isn't mean and doesn't force me to do anything I don't really want to do. He is just determined to do what is in my best interest. He literally fed me like a child when I was hurt and sick. Sometimes he still does and while it should have made me feel uncomfortable like less of an adult, it doesn't. It's his way of showing me just how much he cares for me." I pause to gather my thoughts when Lisa asks what she really wanted to know.

"How's he in bed? I'm assuming it is out of this world." She laughs.

"Definitely. Its mind blowing and I'm not just saying that. It was always nice with David, but Jordan knows his way around the female body. The chemistry between us has always been intense from the moment I first met him, but when we are in bed. I forget everything, but his body on mine. He is a very generous lover. He makes sure I am taken care of first, before he takes any pleasure for himself. It is amazing."

"Damn, now I'm even more jealous." Lisa laughs softly. We talk on for a long time. I finally conversation turns to the pregnancy and the twins. She is still shocked, but happy for us.

"Are you going to be ok starting over at our age? And

twins to boot. Where will you live? You won't be here, will you?" Lisa's voice quivers a little with that last question.

"No, I'll go wherever Jordan is stationed. He thinks we will be back in North Carolina before much longer. It's not so far away. We will be close to the ocean and you can come visit me anytime." I tell her to reassure her our friendship will still be strong despite the distance between us.

After our talk I hang up, I am restless. I wish Jordan, Sr would hurry up and get here. The sound of a car pulling in the drive catches my attention and I hurry to open the door. It's not Jordan, Sr. It's JoAnn. Why is she here? How did she even know that I am here? I walk out to meet her at the bottom of the steps.

"Why are you here?" I demand when she emerges from her car. JoAnn is glaring at me. It's hard to determine what she is thinking from her facial expression.

"I came to see what your plans are, Charlotte. I am not sure why you even came back here." JoAnn says. She moves closer as she awaits my answer.

"I am not sure what you mean JoAnn." I answer quizzically. "I live here. Why wouldn't I come back? My kids live here, my job."

"Poor sweet, Charlotte. You are so naïve. You have always thought the world revolved around you. Haven't you?" JoAnn smirks at me. "All men want you. Patients love you. And you walk around like the fucking Princess everyone treats you as. You have no idea what it's like. Sitting back day after day watching Dr Jones pinning for you. You prance around playing hard to get. I would have been the perfect wife for him. We would have made an awesome power couple, but he only had eyes for you.

Why did you have to come back? That damn meddling Marine. He had to find you and ruin everything."

"What is your problem? Why would you say that to me? I have never done anything to make you say such vile things." I am almost screaming. I am so pissed. Sure Dr. Jones has asked me out in the past, but he wasn't pinning. He's dated other people, surely. Why is she so crazy?

"I had almost gotten him to forget you. Then we get the call that you have been found and you are coming back. He was over the moon happy that you would be coming home. I could not believe my rotten luck. Well now I have made sure you won't ever come back."

"What do you mean?" JoAnn has a crazed look in her eyes. The sound of another vehicle approaching gives me some hope. Please let it be Jordan, Sr. It was not meant to be. Focusing on the SUV coming up the driveway, I don't realize that JoAnn has moved to stand next to me. When the vehicle stops, a couple of Hispanic men climb out, as fear snakes down my spine. A sharp pain pierces my arm. I look down to see a syringe with a milky white substance going into the vein on my forearm, just before the world goes dark.

CHAPTER 27

HAWK

FUCK! Why did this have to come up now. I don't want to leave her. Not while she is vulnerable, pregnant, and scared. She is scared. It was written all over her face. She would never tell me, but I know her. Her body was trembling when I held her before I left. Tears welling in her eyes, but she refused to let them fall. My love for her grows more every damn day. It is imperative I come back home to her, to our babies. I will focus on this mission and get this done, but more every day I am thinking it time to call it quits. I love what I do, but I love her and our family more. Being separated from them for weeks and months at a time is not something I want to be doing anymore. I don't want her worrying about whether or not I am coming back home. It's time I move to a headquarters post. I have been offered one a couple of times but didn't want to give up the field. Now, I am more than ready.

I just have to get to base, ace this mission, then put in for my transfer. Deadeye is ready to take my place in the lead. The guys will be disappointed in me, but it is for the best. It seems to take an eternity to reach base. As soon as we touch down, I head to the briefing room. Captain Olson and the others are already there waiting on me.

"Hawk glad you could make it. Sorry to cut your leave short," Captain Olson smirks when I enter the room.

"I had to finalize some plans first," I reply. I refuse to apologize for making sure Charlotte and the twins were secure before I leave to go on a mission.

"Alright now that the gang is all here. I have a briefing of this mission," Captain Olson begins. "Your job is to get into the palace of the current reigning dignitary of Pakistan rescue the aid workers that have been kidnapped. The press doesn't even know about the aid workers yet. So far, we have been able to keep it quiet. If you can get in, get them, and get back out without anyone being able to identify you, then we win. We will stop international war. The aid workers are really Spies from Russia. If the Russians find out about this, they will declare war and we will have a shit storm on our hands."

"Ok, let's do this. I am ready to get this over with." I declare as I stand ready to head overseas right this minute. Within hours we are loaded up and, on a plane, to take us across the world. I say a silent prayer that we are successful and are back home quickly.

We haven't been in the air long, when it hits me. Something is wrong. I feel it in my heart. Charlotte needs me. Damn I wish I wasn't on a plane going across the globe. Using the satellite phone Captain Olson gave us before we left, I call him. I just need him to confirm that she is with my parents. Olson answers on the 4th ring.

"Olson here." I hear his deep baritone vibrate over the line. He sounds stressed.

"Captain. I need you to do me a favor. Will you call my parents and make sure Charlotte is with them? I know I sound like a worrywart, but I have a bad feeling. I just need confirmation before I am off grid for days on end."

"Umm. I was about to call you. Hawk I don't want you to worry, but Charlotte wasn't at her house when your father arrived. I have sent a team from Fort Campbell out to investigate and your father and brothers are looking as well as her children. We don't have any leads at this point, but we will find her." Olson ends with a heavy sigh.

"Damn it! Where the hell is, she? Has Lopez found her? Tell me what you know," I demand. I need this plane turned around immediately.

"We don't know much. When your dad arrived at her house the front door was standing open, her suitcase was by the door, but she was nowhere to be found. I have sent word for the plane to turn around. You will be back here on base within the hour. As soon as I knew Charlotte was missing, I knew I couldn't send you on that mission," Olson updates me on all he knows.

"Call Tex he's a former SEAL. Wolf knows how to get in touch with him. I have GPS trackers on her at all times. He can find her," I rage into the phone. The need to be on the ground and looking for her is consuming. Normally I would never make such demands of my commanding officer.

"I don't want to know about that do I? I am going to pretend I didn't hear that, but I will call Tex for information. Be safe Hawk and hurry home," Olson ends the call.

"Hawk? What's going on? Is something wrong with

Charlotte? The babies?" Straw asks as all the guys turn to look at me. The concern on their faces helps me to feel slightly better. They care for her too because she is mine.

"She's missing. She wasn't at home when Dad got there. Fuck! I should never have left her there alone."

"Listen, man. You can't blame yourself. She is tough. She will be fine until we can find her," Ace says. "You just found her, no way she is getting away from you that easily."

I know the guys are trying to be reassuring, but it's not helping. I have to get to her. She is still alive. I would know if she were gone, would feel it deep in my soul. It can't happen. I can't live without her. She is my everything, my soulmate. I never believed in such things before especially not for me, but the moment I held her hand in mine in that café, she was mine.

Once we are on the ground, I am running for the command post on base. I need to know every detail of what has happened. When I enter the room, Olson is there looking at map on the wall. Commander Hurt and the SEAL team is there as well.

"Talk to me!" I demand as I enter the room. Ace, Deadeye, Straw, Mercury, Tank, Worm, Virus, Hack, and Wallace on my heels.

"Tex is tracking her. Whoever has her doesn't know about the trackers." Hurt updates me. "They are moving along I-40 toward Texas. We think Lopez's group has her and are attempting to take her back across the border. We are mobilizing teams to head for the border. We will move once we know where they plan to cross."

"I don't want to wait until they get to the damn border. I don't want to imagine what the hell they are doing to her. Damnit, we need to get to her now! She's fucking pregnant with my twins. I can't lose her or them.

It's not an option." I am losing control. I pound my fists on the table. I need to hit something, someone preferably.

"Come on, Hawk. Hold on for Charlotte's sake. She needs you to be calm when we find her," Cookie tells me. I know he is right, but it's hard to keep my cool when I know they are hurting her.

"You know he's right." Deadeye grabs my shoulder. "She's going to be scared. You need to have your shit together so you can calm her fears. If she sees you lose it, there won't be any calmer her down. You got to hang in there, brother." I nod.

"I am sorry. I just need to find her. Sooner rather than later. Let's get ready to head to Texas. I need to be there when we find her." I turn and leave the room, followed by the best group of men a man could ask for as friends and teammates. I know with them helping me, we will find her and bring her home. Hours later we touch down in San Antonio, Texas. I am full of nerves. She is getting closer. I can feel it. Something is definitely going to go down and soon. We have to be ready.

CHAPTER 28

CHARLOTTE

AWARENESS RETURNS SLOWLY. Where am I? I feel a rocking motion and hear the hum of tires on blacktop. I'm in a car. JoAnn injected me with something. Propofol I am certain. Shit! How long have I been out? Oh God! The babies! Are they ok? What is going to happen? Why would JoAnn sedate me? I remember the men getting out of the SUV. Hispanic men. NO! Please no! Don't let it be what I think. She wouldn't help Lopez find me. Would she?

Laying quietly, I pretend that I am still unconscious. There are men talking, but I can't make out what they are saying. Time passes slowly and I drift off again. Dreams of Hawk, our babies, Brian, Sara, and Justin fill the void of my mind. We are all together, happy and a family. Suddenly I am awakened by the careening of the vehicle as it leaves the roadway.

I am thrown around as the vehicle swerves and weaves violently. The men are yelling what I am pretty sure is curse words in Spanish. Sounds of gun fire and the smell of gun powder permeate my nose. What is happening? Where are we? I try to raise my head when the back glass of the SUV shatters. Diving for cover, I wrap my arms over my head, as glass rains down on me. Suddenly the world begins to spin over and over. I am thrown violently around the SUV like a super bouncy ball. I try to curl myself into a ball, but it's almost impossible.

As quickly as it begun, the spinning stops. I am laying on the ceiling of the SUV in a pile of broken glass. Everything hurts. When I raise my head to look around, I hear voices in the distance. Someone is moaning just outside the window on the ground. A man lying in the grass. It's one of my captors. Movement off in the distance catches my eye, the shapes of men are moving in quickly. Please let it be help and not more of these crazed drug dealers.

Hawk

We are so close. Tex has them pinpointed near San Antonio. They were last on I-10. We have created a closure of the interstate, so they are forced to take the route we want. We just have to intercept them before we get too close to the border. We are set up as the SUV approaches. The driver knows the gig is up. He turns the vehicle sharply to avoid the blockage on the road. We move to take chase. He is following into our trap just as we have planned. However, he is a shit driver and dips off the edge of the road a little too far. He can't regain control.

My heart stops when I see the SUV flipping over and over. Charlotte is in there and I doubt they have her belted. It finally comes to a stop. We move in. I have to get to Charlotte. One of the bastards drag her to her feet and begins to back into the trees before we can reach them. I signal for the team to hold their fire.

We can't take a chance on her getting hit in the crossfire.

Charlotte

Suddenly, I am dragged backward out the driver's side of the SUV through the shattered window. Grappling around, I manage to grab hold of a large piece of glass and hold it in my hand. I am pulled to my feet by my hair, not a good sign. A tall muscled man begins to drag me away from the SUV. He has his right arm wrapped around my neck from behind. He is choking me as he drags me off into the surrounding foliage.

"You are too, much trouble, bitch!" He growls into my ear. "I don't know why the boss is so obsessed with getting you back. We should have just killed you. It would have been so much easier. Much less messy. Now I have to kill all those soldiers, which causes more trouble with the US government."

When I stumble, he jerks up hard on my neck. It's a struggle to regain my footing. I really wish I could kill this asshole. The need to find some way to get free burns in my mind. Luckily, I have been able to hold onto the piece of glass. I can use it as a weapon. There is no way I can let him hurt or kill more people. He takes up position behind a large tree. He slams me down at the base of the tree. "Stay put! Or I will gut you." He growls. He continues to scan the horizon in front of us. He is looking for an opportunity to shoot whomever caused us to crash.

Hawk

We continue to move in closer, keeping his attention on us. Unknown to the madman that has Charlotte, I have men moving in from behind as well. We just have to wait for the right moment to make our move. Time moves by slowly. Ace signals that the second team is in position. Ok, time to make a push to draw his attention our way, while they overtake him from behind. I take aim but shoot wide. I must be sure the shots are nowhere close to Charlotte.

Charlotte

This is not going to be easy. I'll need to be creative. It will be necessary to wait until he is distracted enough that I can stab him. I need to go for the throat. It will be the easiest way to take him out. I am not sure if I have enough strength or skill to hit his heart or lungs. He is barely paying any attention to me, so I watch him carefully waiting for the perfect moment to make my move. Taking a couple of deep breaths to get the courage to do what has to be done, I see him raise his pistol and take aim. This is my opportunity, while he is distracted.

I leap to my feet, but he sees me and swings at me. I duck out of the way just in time. He faulters when he misses making contact with my face. I pop back to my feet and make to fatal slash across his throat, while he is off balance. Blood spatters across my face. The man grabs his throat and begins to fall backwards as he drops his gun. The sound of the gun going off and a flash of fire registers in my brain as the bullet leaves the barrel. Searing pain rocks my body and I lose my footing. The ground comes up to smack me hard. I've been shot.

Hawk

The kidnapper fires in our direction. A shout rings out as the man swing his arm around to hit Charlotte. She is standing next to him with something in her hand. Is that blood dripping from her hand? I try to shout, to warn her to get back before he hits her. At the last second, she ducks. His swing is wide, and he stumbles. Charlotte is on her feet again. She slashes across the man's throat. He falls back dropping his gun. The gun fires as it hits the ground. Charlotte drops like a rock. “NO!” tears from my lips as I break into a dead run.

Charlotte

Please God, let my babies survive this. I can’t lose them, not now. Hawk was so happy. It would destroy him. He is all about family. It was easy to see in the time I spent with him and his family. God the pain is all consuming. The metallic taste of blood floods my mouth as I cough. I never knew getting shot hurt so damn bad. Help is coming. I saw them before I was shot. Hawk is among them. I can feel he is close. I have to hang on just a little longer.

Warm arms wrap around me. Looking up I see Hawk’s beautiful green eyes boring into me with concern. I reach up to touch his gorgeously handsome face. Everything will be right with the world, now. Hawk is here. He found me. I knew he would. How he is here I have no idea. He was being sent on a mission. He should be far away from here by this time. God does answer prayers. I prayed he would find us and here he is holding me in his arms. He is carrying me somewhere.

“Charlotte, love. Hold on for me. Help is coming.” Hawk looks frantic. Fear floods me, now. I have never seen him afraid. The look on his face right now is terrifying. “Please don’t leave me, love. I need you. I love you so fucking much. I need you to be here with me.” I hear his voice crack. He is running, yelling for medics. I feel so light. The light is dimming. Is it night already? Why can’t I see him anymore?

CHAPTER 29

HAWK

Oh God! This is bad. She is so pale. There is too much blood. I am running on instinct. I have to get her to the medics. We have to stop the bleeding. An ambulance on the road waiting for us. Screaming for help, I have no idea what I am saying. They just need to help her. The twins won't survive this. There is way too much blood. I will grieve them, but I cannot lose her. A medic rips her from my arms and lays her on a stretcher. She isn't looking at me. Her eyes are vacant, and half closed. She can't die. I won't let her. I vow as they are working on her.

Ace and Mercury are pulling me back. They are telling me I have to give the medics room to work, but I need to touch her. I must keep in contact with her. Somehow, I know it will keep her here with me. She needs the contact to help her hold on to me. The sounds of a chopper approaching gives me some hope. It is coming to land on the road behind us. The medics move to take her to the chopper and I follow never letting my hold falter.

It only takes minutes to reach the trauma center. The doctor is waiting on the helipad. He tells us that the OR is ready. We head straight there. They intend to make me stop at the door, but I refuse. I will not let her go under any circumstances. Captain Olson has made arrangements to give us special access. Ace convinces them to don me in surgical scrubs and let me sit at her head. It is totally not protocol, but I need to be here. Whatever happens today I need to be here with her. She needs my strength.

The surgery seems to take forever. They work franticly to stop the bleeding. She was hit in the right lower chest. It got her bad lung and nicked the liver. They are giving her transfusions during the surgery. After what seems an eternity, they are closing her up. The doctor says they have done all they can do.

Later we are moved to ICU. So far, the twins are doing fine. Strong heartbeats. Their mother is holding her own as well. There are so many damn tubes. IV's, chest tube, ventilator, and more I don't have names for at the moment. She is the strongest woman I know. She has been kidnapped, in a rollover MVA, and shot, yet she is still hanging on to life and to our babies. Captain Olson is working on getting our family here. I have talked to my parents and son and I reassured her children that she would be fine.

Hours later, the gang arrives. I am still parked at her bedside. Sara and Justin enter the room. The worry and fear in their eyes is easy to see. It is a mirror of my own emotions. This woman is what holds our family together. Without her it will all fall apart. Brian comes in, too. He looks unsure of himself as he nears the bed. So, I reach for his hand. He comes to my side.

"How is she, Dad?" Brian is whispering so quiet I can hardly hear him.

"She is hanging on, son. She just needs time to heal. She will be with us soon." I tell him with conviction. Sara rounds the bed and comes up to us. I can tell she is nervous, and I want to reassure her that Charlotte will be fine soon. I have to believe it. There is no other option for me.

"Umm...Brian? I am Sara and this is Justin." Sara says as she gestures behind her to her brother. "We are Charlotte's children. It's good to meet you. I just wish it wasn't here like this. I know you don't know us, but Mom wanted us to be a family. I hope you can come to think of us as your family. No matter what happens with Mom." Sara finishes as her voices hitches as she tries to hold back the tears that are brimming in her eyes.

"Hello, Sara, Justin." Brian says as he shakes their hands. "I would like that, but Charlotte is going to be fine. So, don't talk about what she wants in the past tense." Sara nods in agreement even though her eyes tell a different story.

I am so proud of the young man Brian is becoming. His faith is exceeding my own. I have been on edge since the moment I saw her hit the ground. My heart stopped beating. I have been in limbo, waiting for the smallest sign that the woman I love is coming back to me. Thought beyond this moment is impossible. Each second, she's unconscious is an eternity of torture. We set up vigil and wait. The hours pass by slowly. The longer she is out the harder it is for me to hold onto hope.

CHAPTER 30

HAWK

DAMN I SURE HURT. What happened? Where am I? The memories come flooding back with a vengeance. I was kidnapped and we wrecked. Then I killed that man and as his dying act he shot me. Oh No! the babies! Are they ok? Did I lose them? Where is Hawk? He is close. I can feel it in my heart he is with me, so I open my eyes to look around. The room is quiet and dark. A slight glow from the heart monitor over my bed glows softly. A warm hand takes mine. Looking to my left, all my anxiety leaves me. Hawk is there, looking into my eyes. I try to smile at him, and he returns the gesture.

"Hi." I try to whisper, but the tube down my throat makes it impossible. Coughs rack my body and an alarm begins to sound near the bed. A ventilator. I force myself to stop fighting the machine.

"Hi, love" Hawk's face softens and relaxes. My last memory of him was a look of sheer terror on his face. Fear for me, our babies. Fear that we would never get our happily ever after. Worry for our babies again consumes me. Laying my hand on my stomach, I raise my eyes to his in question.

"They are doing fine, love. They are strong just like their mother." Hawk comes sit on the bed next to me and places his hand over mine on my stomach. Relief floods me. They are alive. Medical personnel come in and out of the room checking equipment and reset the alarms. When I am fully awake, the doctors come in and remove the tube from my throat. Being able to breath on my own, I whisper hoarsely.

"You are the most amazing woman I have ever had the pleasure of knowing. I love you, so much. Please don't scare me like that again. I can't live my life without you." Hawk tells me when the doctor and nurses have left us alone.

"I am so sorry that I scared you. I can't believe that it happened to me again. I love you so much. I was so afraid I would never see you again. Afraid I would lose our babies. I am sorry that I let myself be kidnapped again..." I rattle on as I try hard to convey everything running through my mind. Hawk places his index finger over my lips.

"Love you have nothing to be sorry for. You made it through, and you kept our babies safe. I am so damn proud of you, of your strength. I can't wait to marry you. I need to make you mine."

"I'm yours, Hawk. From the moment you took my hand in that café, I have been yours. There will never be anyone, but you for me." Hawk takes my hand and kisses it gently.

Suddenly the room is astir. Our family and friends flood the room. Everyone is talking at the same time. I am so happy to have everyone around me, supporting us. We are so blessed.

Hopefully this nightmare is over. I need to tell them about JoAnn's part in my abduction. Once all the chatter has settled down, I inquire about what happened while I was out. Captain Olson informs us they were able to link JoAnn to the drug runners. She has been arrested. A SEAL team along with a group of Marine Special Ops have apprehended Hugo Lopez and his Asshole brother. Their drug dealing, gun running, and forced prostitution days are over.

After several days in the hospital, I am released to go home. I just have to decide where home is located. I want to be wherever Hawk is. For now, we are headed back to California and the Naval base. It's time for my follow up with Dr Martin. It is almost laughable since I was in ICU with a team of doctors and nurses checking me and the twins constantly. But I need this, to get back some semblance of normalcy.

A few days later, after getting a good report from Dr Martin, we head back to our house on base. My kids and Hawk's family will be here this weekend to visit. I am so looking forward to us all being together. We will be a family again. I can't wait. We are inviting Hawk's friends and co-workers over as well. It will be one epic party. Hawk says everyone wants to celebrate my release from the hospital and the end of my nightmare at the hands of my former friend JoAnn and 2 psychopathic drug runners.

Saturday arrives and the house is abuzz with activity. Hawk's brothers are in the backyard with Deadeye and Ace manning the grill. Hawk's Mom, Diane has been hovering over me since she arrived. Currently she is fussing over my hair. For some reason she has decided I needed a special hairdo for the picnic. Sara is helping and they seem to be having a bonding moment. I let them pamper me. It's the least I can do right? They seem so happy, no need to spoil the moment.

I am wearing the most beautiful new dress. Hawk picked it out himself. It is a lovely cream color. It is form fitting at the top and flares out from just under my breasts and falls to my knees, hiding the bump forming in my lower abdomen. A lavender sash hits just under my breasts and there is lavender lace around the hem. A pair of white flats rounds out the ensemble. Diane has pulled the sides of my hair back in little braids and has secured them behind my head. Sara has put small white and lavender flowers in my braids. There is a light layer of makeup on my face. My lips and cheeks a light shade of mauve. I am feeling better than I had for a while, but I am still nervous about getting sick when I smell the food.

I am feeling antsy. Hawk hasn't been around all day. He left before I woke, and he's been MIA all day. He has text me and assured me he is fine just catching up on work and setting up for the picnic. Once I am dressed, Hawk's sister Danica knocks on our bedroom door. She informs us that everyone is waiting for us to come out. I frown, not understanding why people would be waiting on us. Diane and Sara plant a quick kiss on my cheek, and they hurry from the room.

I walk down the short hallway and realize not a soul is in the house. Everyone is already outside. Before I can step out the door, Hawk is there. He inhales sharply as his eyes rove over my body. I feel as if he has stripped me naked in front of everyone. He stalks to me with his sexy body of muscles that flex and ripple as he moves toward me. He has the most intense gaze as he looks at me with his beautiful green eyes that I get lost in. He takes my hand and places a soft kiss on my palm.

He is the most gorgeous man I have ever had the pleasure to lay eyes on. He has the body of Adonis and despite the layers of clothes he has on today, he can't hide it. He is wearing a brown sport coat over a lavender dress shirt that is the same shade of my dress. His brown dress pants hug his muscled thighs and firm butt cheeks. His hair and beard look freshly trimmed. An image of him between my thighs with my juices sparkling in his beard flashes in my mind.

"Charlotte love, you are so lovely in that dress. You have stolen my breath along with my heart. I asked all our friends and family to be here today, because I want to marry you today." Hawk declares as he leads me out into the back yard where they have set up chairs, a small stage, and an arch for us to be married under. Everything is decorated in lavender and white. "I hope you are ok with this small ceremony in front of our closest friends and family. I didn't want to waste another day. I want you to be my wife and have my name."

Overcome with emotion, tears flood my eyes. I can't believe that he has pulled this whole thing off without me finding out. The crowd that has gathered is absolutely perfect. Our families is here and our friends. Even Lisa my oldest friend is here. I couldn't have imagined a more perfect setting. Train's *Marry Me* begins to play in the background. I turn to look at the man that has stolen my heart, too. With tears in my eyes, I ask.

"What are we waiting for? Let's get this party started." My face beaming with a smile. Hawk takes my hand and leads me to the altar. The minister begins the ceremony, but I don't hear a word. All my focus is on Hawk's beautiful green eyes and the love I see reflected back at me. I am so in love with him. I never dreamed I would have this, us, our family.

Hawk squeezes my hand; I look at him quizzically. He shifts his eyes toward the minister. The minister is awaiting my response. Apparently, he has asked me a question while I was lost in his eyes. I look to the minister questioningly and feel a blush flush my face. The crowd chuckles. The minister repeats himself.

"Do you Charlotte Ruth Williams, take Jordan Brian Jackson, II to be your lawfully wedded husband? To have and to hold, for richer, or poorer, in sickness and health, in good times and bad times, until death do you part?"

"I do." I reply. Happiness abounds in my heart.

"Do you Jordan Brian Jackson, II take Charlotte Ruth Williams to be your lawfully wedded wife?" To have and to hold, for richer, or poorer, in sickness and health, in good times and bad times, until death do you part?"

"I do" Jordan says. Tears are welling in his eyes.

"With the power vested in me by the State of California, I now pronounce you husband and wife. You may kiss your bride." The minister declares.

Hawk reverently takes my face in his hands. He leans in and places his lips on mine. It is gentle, tender. He licks at my lips and I open in response. He deeps the kiss. My arms snake around his waist and I pull him close. I am lost in the moment. I think he is lost as well. We are brought back to awareness as the minister clears his throat. Hawk pulls back reluctantly with a huge grin on his face. I blush profusely. The crowd cheers. We turn to face the crowd.

"Ladies and Gentlemen, I present Mr. and Mrs. Jordan Brian Jackson, II."

We walk down the aisle while everyone cheers and throws birdseed at us. I squeal with delight as Hawk sweeps me off my feet and carries me back to the house. We are having the reception here so why we went into the house is beyond me, but he seems to be in a hurry to get me to our room. I am laughing hysterically by the time we reach it. Hawk is laughing, too. He rushes inside the room and turns to lock the door behind us.

"What are you doing?" I exclaim. "We have guests waiting on us."

"They can wait. We need to consummate this marriage." Hawk declares as he unzips my dress.

"Are you serious?" I am giggling like a schoolgirl. "You are so bad."

"No, I am SOOO good. You have told me many, many times as you scream my name while you are under me, covered in sweat. Your face flushed from our love making. I need to see and hear that now." Hawk is undressing me and himself while he is talking.

"I love you, Jordan Brian Hawk Jackson." I gush as he pushes me back onto the bed. I am fully naked now and so is he. He crawls onto the bed with me as I lay back on the pillows. I reach up and grab his neck to pull him down to me. Hawk closes the distance and lowers his mouth to mine. The kiss is searing. It is deep, sensuous. He breaks the kiss and moves to kiss down my jaw to my ear. He nibbles on my earlobe and whispers in my ear.

"You are the most beautiful woman I have ever seen. I swear I see Heaven when I look at you."

I shiver from his whispered words in my ear. He moves to kiss down my neck. I moan as he sucks my left nipple in his mouth. His mouth is hot, moist. His tongue flicks my nipple and his teeth close on it to tug gently. My hands are in his hair encouraging him to continue. I arch into him. He moves to the right and repeats his actions. Wetness is pooling between my thighs.

My hands rove over his bare muscular shoulders. God, he feels so good. I love everything about him.

Wanting to convey to him all that I am feeling through our love making, I move to sit up. I push him back onto the mattress as I straddle him. I kiss him deeply then move my way down his body. He shudders under my mouth when I suck on his nipple. I nibble my way down his muscular chest to the v that drops down to his manhood.

His hard, muscular length throbs between us. I take him in my hands and stroke him, from head to base and back. Gripping his base firmly, I lower my mouth to lick the head. Umm he tastes so good. I suck him inside my mouth and take as much as I can. He fists his hands in my hair. The large head of his cock bumps the back of my throat and still I try to take more. Slowly I slide my mouth back up his length, sucking and swirling my tongue around his shaft. I go down again, sucking gently then hard, constantly alternating the pressure as I work him in and out of my mouth. Moving faster and faster, bringing him closer to the edge.

Suddenly, he jerks up sharply on my head. A pop resounds as I break suction. I look to him questioningly.

"I need to come inside you, love. If I didn't stop you, I would come in your mouth." Hawk states huskily.

"I want to taste you, baby." I say honestly with a little whine. I move to go back to my task.

"Later, love. I promise, but first I want you." Hawk demands.

"You are so bossy. Always getting your way." I laugh as he flips me onto my back. My laugh becomes a gasp as he sucks my clit into his mouth, and he begins to nip and lick. He slides two fingers inside me and pumps feverishly. "Oh God, Hawk! It's too much. I... oh God! No! Don't stop!" He adds a third finger and continues to suck on my clit. The orgasm building in my core. I buck my hips to meet his thrusts. He moans against my mouth and it pushes me over the edge. I quiver and scream his name over and over, but still he continues to assault me. Once I am coming back to earth, he raises his head and licks his lips.

He smiles at me as he makes his way back to my mouth. He kisses me deeply. I can taste myself on his tongue. "You like how good you taste, love? I can't get enough. Are you ready for me? I need to be inside you, riding you hard."

"Yes, Hawk. I am more than ready. Give it to me." I say as I spread my legs wider to give him the best access. He runs his fingers through my folds and rubs my juices on the head of his cock. He nestles it into my opening. I arch up to meet him as he slides into me. All the way to the hilt. He feels so good inside me. I love how he knows just how to move to bring me to the brink. His long hard length is just right. It fits inside me just right. It is like we were made for each other. He slings my legs up over his shoulders as he begins to pound in and out of me.

Hawk

Fuck! My woman is so responsive. She responses to my every touch, every move. She gives as good as she gets, though. I was almost lost in the moment of her mouth on me and almost let her get me off, before I took her. But I needed to be inside her and hear her come, the noises she makes are divine. I love this woman more than I ever thought possible. My love grows every day. And that just makes the passion better. The need to move in and out of her faster and faster drives me. Her legs are thrown up over my shoulders. She meets my every thrust by arching her hips up so I can get deeper. So, I give her what she needs. Harder, faster, more. My orgasm is building, and I am about to come as my balls draw up. I reach between us and put just the right amount of pressure on her clit. Circling my thumb faster as I continue to pump in and out of her moist, hot sex. Her walls begin to flutter, and she explodes on my cock, I thrust again and again, until I am coming inside her. My seed is shooting out stream after stream. Complete at last, I ease down onto the bed and roll us until she is laying at my side. I place a kiss on her head as she settles her head on my chest.

We are panting hard. She still quivers from her orgasm. Gently my hand runs over her bare back, stroking her, settling her. I try to catch my breath to tell her how much she means to me. How she has made me the happiest man on the earth. I never thought I would find this peace, happiness, contentment.

"Charlotte, I love you. You have given me more than I ever thought would be possible for me. I never thought I could love like this. I didn't realize what I was missing until I met you at that café. I am so very thankful you spoke to me that day and while I hate what you had to endure; I thank God that I was the one who found you in the jungle."

"Oh Jordan, I am thankful, too. I thought I would never love again. I had resigned myself to live alone the rest of my life. Then you took my hand in that café and my life began again. It was horrible what I went through in the jungle, but it was worth all the pain and suffering. It brought you to me in the end. We are here together, and we are going to have a wonderful family. I love you, Jordan Jackson."

"Let's get out there to our party, love. The guests are going to wonder where we are." I chuckle. Life is just getting good; I can't wait to see the rest of our life together.

EPILOGUE

Hawk

One year later....

I wake to the sounds of retching coming from the bathroom. Looking to my right I see I am again alone in the bed. That is the third time this week. Slipping out of the bed to head for the bathroom, I pause at the baby monitor on the bedside table and see the twins are still sleeping. Upon entering the bathroom, Charlotte on her knees in front of the toilet. Kneeling next to her, I wipe her hair back. She is awfully pale, and a thin sheer of sweat is on her brow.

"Charlotte, love. Are you alright?" I ask her.

"Yeah, I'm feeling better now. I must have eaten something that didn't agree with me." She sighs. I rise and get a washcloth. After wetting it, I place it on her forehead. She leans into me. I slip my arms under her and pick her up and carry her back to bed. It's still early, the twins won't be up for a while maybe. I ease her down on the mattress and look into her gorgeous eyes.

"Charlotte, I don't think you ate something that upset your stomach. That is the third morning this week." I look at her questioningly.

"Hawk, what are you thinking?" Charlotte asks me, as she frowns in thought. I reach out and run my hands over her breasts. She winces and pulls away.

"Have you been dizzy? Taking naps in the afternoon?" I question. "You and I both know what is wrong with you, love." Smiling at her like a goofy teenage boy, seeing his girlfriend naked for the first time. I am overwhelmed with excitement. We are going to ride the baby roller coaster again. Hopefully there will only be one this time.

"Hawk, you think I'm pregnant again?" Charlotte asks me with wide eyes.

"Yes, love. I see all the signs. We haven't used protection or birth control. We wanted more kids, right?" I am concerned now. What if she isn't ok with this? I know it's awfully quick, but we are older and if we are going to have more now is the time.

"Yes. Oh my! I just didn't even think of it. I have been so absorbed in the boys. I didn't even consider we could be pregnant again. I'm nursing that's supposed to prevent pregnancy at least for a while." Charlotte says. I can see the emotions running across her face. Suddenly she stops and a huge smile spreads across her face. "We are going to be parents again!"

"Yes, love. We are." I reply as I hear the first stirring cries of our sons. Getting out of bed to slip on my sweatpants, I tell her. "I'll be right back with our boys." I turn and leave the room only to return a few moments later with our sons, one in each arm. "Think the boys are hungry, love."

Charlotte is settled on the bed and ready for them. I

lay Joshua on her right side and help her get him into position as he begins to suckle. Once he is settled. I position Jessie on her left side propping him with pillows. I love to watch my boys feeding from their mother's glorious breasts. I love that she nourishes them with her milk. We have the perfect life. No everything isn't perfect, but us with our kids, all of them. That is perfect.

Things have changed a lot in the last year. Besides the birth of the twins, I was promoted to Captain and I am in charge of the headquarters division of the team now. We are stationed at Camp Lejeune, NC. Brain chose to move here with us. He is a senior in high school this year. He has so much potential. He's smart, funny, and very perceptive. He has discussed enlisting. He knows that Charlotte and I will support any decision he makes. I would like for him to go to college and have a normal boring life, but I realize it's in his blood as well as his name. All the Jordan Brian Jacksons have joined the service. I know it is inevitable he will do the same.

Sara and Justin come to visit at least once a month. They have been so supportive and helpful to their mother. Sara stayed for 2 weeks after the boys were born. She helped take care of them and keep the house running while Charlotte and I adjusted to being new parents. My parents visit often, and Mom has loved helping with the boys.

Dad seems pleased that I have moved up in rank and I'm no longer being sent into the middle of danger. I knew I had to take on this roll for Charlotte and our family. For too long I have caused them worry and fear. I am surprisingly satisfied in my new roll. I go to base every day and come home to Charlotte and our sons every night. We go to Brian's events at school as a family.

It is the best life. And now it seems we will be adding a new addition to the mix.

The team stops by from time to time. Deadeye is now in charge in the field. He still seeks out my friendship and advice. The team is leaving today on a top-secret mission. It will be one of the toughest they have ever faced, but they are up for the task. However, I can't help but feel some trepidation. It feels like this mission will change everything, for the team. I need to be there for them.

* * *

Deadeye

WE ARE HEADING out for the middle East. I have an uneasy feeling about this one. It feels like my life is about to change fundamentally. I'm not sure what is coming, but I know that I must be at my upmost best. I have to keep my teammates safe at all costs as I am responsible for all of them. Now I know what Hawk has dealt with all these years. The weight of responsibility is overwhelming, but I know I was trained by the best and I will be successful. It is what I was born to do.

We land in Afghanistan at a secure base. We head to the hanger to get an update on the situation. An aide worker has gone missing at the refugee camp. It is our task to find out where she is and get her out if possible. The latest intelligence reports indicate that she was taken about 24 hours ago as she was traveling in a convoy making its way from one side of the refugee camp to the other with supplies. The guards and interrupter were shot dead at the scene. A female worker, Elise Sommers, had not been heard from since.

At the briefing we learn there have been some developments as we traveled here. A rumor is that she has been taken into the desert. One of ISIS leaders, Omadir Hussan is planning on making her his bride. He has released a statement that she is unharmed and well cared for. She was seen on video stating that she is happy and requests that no one try to find her. She chose to leave with Omadir, who will soon be her husband.

Something about the woman, touched me when I saw her in that video. She spoke clearly, her voice never wavering. She was quite convincing, but it was her eyes that gave away what she was really feeling. They were full of fear and desperation. She never chose to be there, but she would endure whatever came her way in an effort to prevent any more deaths. Her eyes haunt me.

That is why this mission is so important. I have to get her out before that bastard can force her to marry him and rape her. We ready our packs, study the large map in the command post, and are headed into the desert in a few short hours. Time is ticking and Elise is counting on us to get her to safety. I can feel it.

ABOUT THE AUTHOR

Angela Rush is a wife, mother, grandmother and full time nurse practitioner. She lives in southern rural Kentucky with her husband.

This is Angela's debut manuscript.

facebook.com/angela.rush.167

There are many more books in this fan fiction world than listed here, for an up-to-date list go to www.AcesPress.com

You can also visit our Amazon page at: http://www.amazon.com/author/operationalpha

Special Forces: Operation Alpha World

Denise Agnew: Dangerous to Hold
Shauna Allen: Awakening Aubrey
Shauna Allen: Defending Danielle
Shauna Allen: Rescuing Rebekah
Shauna Allen: Saving Scarlett
Shauna Allen: Saving Grace
Brynne Asher: Blackburn
Jennifer Becker: Hiding Catherine
Julia Bright: Saving Lorelei
Julia Bright: Rescuing Amy
Victoria Bright: Surviving Savage
Victoria Bright: Going Ghost
Victoria Bright: Jostling Joker
Cara Carnes: Protecting Mari
Kendra Mei Chailyn: Beast
Kendra Mei Chailyn: Barbie
Kendra Mei Chailyn : Pitbull
Melissa Kay Clarke: Rescuing Annabeth
Melissa Kay Clarke: Safeguarding Miley
Samantha A. Cole: Handling Haven
Samantha A. Cole: Cheating the Devil
Sue Coletta: Hacked
Melissa Combs: Gallant
KaLyn Cooper: Rescuing Melina
Liz Crowe: Marking Mariah
Jordan Dane: Redemption for Avery

Jordan Dane: Fiona's Salvation
Riley Edwards: Protecting Olivia
Riley Edwards: Redeeming Violet
Riley Edwards, Recovering Ivy
Nicole Flockton: Protecting Maria
Nicole Flockton: Guarding Erin
Nicole Flockton: Guarding Suzie
Nicole Flockton: Guarding Brielle
Casey Hagen: Shielding Nebraska
Casey Hagen: Shielding Harlow
Casey Hagen: Shielding Josie
Casey Hagen: Shielding Blair
Desiree Holt: Protecting Maddie
Kathy Ivan: Saving Sarah
Kathy Ivan: Saving Savannah
Kathy Ivan: Saving Stephanie
Jesse Jacobson: Protecting Honor
Jesse Jacobson: Fighting for Honor
Jesse Jacobson: Defending Honor
Jesse Jacobson: Summer Breeze
Silver James: Rescue Moon
Silver James: SEAL Moon
Silver James: Assassin's Moon
Silver James: Under the Assassin's Moon
Becca Jameson: Saving Sofia
Kate Kinsley: Protecting Ava
Heather Long: Securing Arizona
Heather Long: Guarding Gertrude
Heather Long: Protecting Pilar
Heather Long: Covering Coco
Gennita Low: No Protection
Kirsten Lynn: Joining Forces for Jesse
Margaret Madigan: Bang for the Buck
Margaret Madigan: Buck the System

Margaret Madigan: Jungle Buck
Margaret Madigan: December Chill
Rachel McNeely: The SEAL's Surprise Baby
Rachel McNeely: The SEAL's Surprise Bride
Rachel McNeely: The SEAL's Surprise Twin
KD Michaels: Saving Laura
KD Michaels: Protecting Shane
KD Michaels: Avenging Angels
Wren Michaels: The Fox & The Hound
Wren Michaels: The Fox & The Hound 2
Wren Michaels: Shadow of Doubt
Wren Michaels: Shift of Fate
Wren Michaels: Steeling His Heart
Kat Mizera: Protecting Bobbi
Mary B Moore: Force Protection
LeTeisha Newton: Protecting Butterfly
LeTeisha Newton: Protecting Goddess
LeTeisha Newton: Protecting Vixen
LeTeisha Newton: Protecting Heartbeat
MJ Nightingale: Protecting Beauty
MJ Nightingale: Betting on Benny
MJ Nightingale: Protecting Secrets
Sarah O'Rourke: Saving Liberty
Debra Parmley: Protecting Pippa
Debra Parmley: Split Screen Scream
Lainey Reese: Protecting New York
Jenika Snow: Protecting Lily
Jen Talty: Burning Desire
Jen Talty: Burning Kiss
Jen Talty: Burning Skies
Jen Talty: Burning Lies
Jen Talty: Burning Heart
Megan Vernon: Protecting Us
Megan Vernon: Protecting Earth

Police and Fire: Operation Alpha World

Freya Barker: Burning for Autumn
KaLyn Cooper: Justice for Gwen
Aspen Drake: Sheltering Emma
Deanndra Hall: Shelter for Sharla
Deanndra Hall:Justice for Aleta
Barb Han: Kace
Reina Torres: Justice for Sloane
Stacey Wilk: Stage Fright

As you know, this book included at least one character from Susan Stoker's books. To check out more, see below.

SEAL of Protection: Legacy Series

Securing Caite
Securing Brenae (novella)
Securing Sidney
Securing Piper
Securing Zoey (Jan 2020)
Securing Avery (May 2020)
Securing Kalee (Sept 2020)

Delta Team Two Series

Shielding Gillian (Apr 2020)
Shielding Kinley (Aug 2020)
Shielding Aspen (Oct 2020)
Shielding Riley (TBA)
Shielding Devyn (TBA)
Shielding Ember (TBA)
Shielding Sierra (TBA)

Delta Force Heroes Series

Rescuing Rayne (FREE!)
Rescuing Aimee (novella)
Rescuing Emily
Rescuing Harley
Marrying Emily (novella)
Rescuing Kassie
Rescuing Bryn
Rescuing Casey
Rescuing Sadie (novella)
Rescuing Wendy
Rescuing Mary

Rescuing Macie (Novella)

Badge of Honor: Texas Heroes Series

Justice for Mackenzie (FREE!)
Justice for Mickie
Justice for Corrie
Justice for Laine (novella)
Shelter for Elizabeth
Justice for Boone
Shelter for Adeline
Shelter for Sophie
Justice for Erin
Justice for Milena
Shelter for Blythe
Justice for Hope
Shelter for Quinn
Shelter for Koren
Shelter for Penelope

SEAL of Protection Series

Protecting Caroline (FREE!)
Protecting Alabama
Protecting Fiona
Marrying Caroline (novella)
Protecting Summer
Protecting Cheyenne
Protecting Jessyka
Protecting Julie (novella)
Protecting Melody
Protecting the Future
Protecting Kiera (novella)
Protecting Alabama's Kids (novella)
Protecting Dakota

New York Times, USA Today and *Wall Street Journal* Bestselling Author Susan Stoker has a heart as big as the state of Tennessee where she lives, but this all American girl has also spent the last fourteen years living in Missouri, California, Colorado, Indiana, and Texas. She's married to a retired Army man who now gets to follow *her* around the country.

www.stokeraces.com
www.AcesPress.com
susan@stokeraces.com

Made in the USA
Monee, IL
21 April 2024